Robert T Morris

Hopkin's Pond and Other Sketches

Robert T Morris

Hopkin's Pond and Other Sketches

ISBN/EAN: 9783337095635

Printed in Europe, USA, Canada, Australia, Japan

Cover: Foto ©Andreas Hilbeck / pixelio.de

More available books at **www.hansebooks.com**

HOPKINS'S POND

AND

OTHER SKETCHES

BY

ROBERT T. MORRIS

G. P. PUTNAM'S SONS

NEW YORK LONDON
27 WEST TWENTY-THIRD STREET 24 BEDFORD STREET, STRAND
The Knickerbocker Press
1896

DEDICATED TO
THE MEMORY OF MY BELOVED FATHER
LUZON B. MORRIS
WHO ENJOYED EVERYTHING THAT HIS
CHILDREN ENJOYED

PREFACE.

WHEN these sketches were first published, the author had no more thought of preserving them in book form, than the brown thrush thinks of recording the things that he says to his mate from the bending tip-top of a white birch in June. They were penned in spare moments to please the little coterie of friends who gather about my open fireplace in the long winter evenings, where the largest bass fails to escape from the hook, and where the bear makes his most furious onslaught. There was a pleasure also in fixing certain thoughts in definite form so that when fatigued with work and with city surroundings I could turn to an old paper and find that I really had thought of nice things once.

Then again there was a feeling that the

pappus of the pen might float a tiny bit of germ to some barren office desk, where it would spring into fresh memories for some lover of richer fields, who was chained to the desk.

Many sketches which were published anonymously and in various places have been trimmed out of mind by the sickle of the Reaper, and I do not know where to look for them to-day, but the Editor of *Forest and Stream* has found in his files a number of contributions that were published over my name, or over the *nom de plume* of Mark West, which was adopted from the familiar call of New England sea-shooters. The story from the sandy end of a Connecticut township was published in *The Rider and Driver*.

CONTENTS.

	PAGE
HOPKINS'S POND	1
BONASA UMBELLUS, REX	17
THE AUTOCRAT OF THE EDDY	40
WATCHING THE BRANT GROW BIG	53
THE LAIR OF SOMETHING STRIPED	71
SUCKER DAYS	78
THE EVENING OF AUGUST 1, 1895	89
IN THE SANDY END OF A CONNECTICUT TOWNSHIP	105
A DAY WITH THE GROUSE	118
THE NEPIGON AND SAGUENAY RIVERS	128
THE NUMBER NINE AS A TALE VARNISHER,	141
EN KLAPJAGT PAA DANSKE FJELDE	151
ONE DEER	176
A BIT OF GROUSE-HUNTER'S LORE	185
TROUT IN A THUNDER-STORM	199

Contents.

PAGE

COOT SHOOTING IN NEW ENGLAND . . 204

RUFFED GROUSE AMONG THE GRAPE-VINES . 207

WING SHOOTING VERSUS GROUND SHOOTING 212

MY WHITE VIOLET—POETRY . . 218

AN EASTER CROCUS—POETRY . . . 219

THE EMPTY KENNEL—POETRY . . . 220

THE OLD-SQUAW—POETRY 224

WHAT I FOUND IN THE HUNTING-COAT

POCKET—POETRY 226

HOPKINS'S POND
AND OTHER SKETCHES

HOPKINS'S POND.

ECHO hiding up among the rocks quietly reproved the boy who yelled too loudly when he pulled the croaking bullhead out of the warm pond water, and with a low, forbearing voice showed with nice modulation how the sound of joy ought to be made next time.

It was a quiet pond, without a single bad trait, excepting that it smelled rather pondy in summer when the water was low, but that is nothing to a boy. Its tranquillity was in keeping with the tranquil farms that extended part way around it, but it nevertheless had certain subdued sounds of its own, for in the spring the honest toad sat in a leaky bog and trilled a serenade to his love who was largely immersed in the cool water below. Little frogs chuckled and big frogs rumbled in

bass, while the old mill wheel, which la-
bored irregularly, mingled its thumpings
with the sound of water plunging over the
low wooden dam.   Such sounds were very
different, though, from the rattle and
bang of a noisy engine and the screech of
a steam saw that one is in danger of hearing nowadays if he is not judicious about
his selection of ponds.   We never heard
anything of that sort about old-fashioned
Hopkins's Pond, which was very dear to
the heart of the boy, and very dreadful in
the mind of his mother, who imagined
that its eager depths were always yawning
for her dirty little darling, who had safely
outgrown the cistern and the well.

As a matter of fact, it was about as good
a pond as one could imagine, though it
really was rather deep, down by the flume
where the water silently moved under-
ground in a slow, portentous current, and
the sticks and rusty bait boxes that we
boys threw in there disappeared forever.
If such things went as completely out of
sight in the bonfire in the garden it was
a different matter.   When the agrostis

ghosts and dead leaves had all been raked
out from under the currant bushes and
piled upon the heap of trimmings from
the grapevines and apple trees, a cloud
of crackling smoke rolled up into the
balmy spring air that was more fitted to
receive the bluebird's song, and into the
fire we threw various garden rakings : a
tail from a wornout buffalo-robe, and a
heavy dried paint-pot, a chicken's foot, a
recently unearthed spool that little sister
begged us to spare for her wagon, a piece
of bagging with plaster on it, the remnant
of a hoop-skirt, an old tow chignon that
the pup had dragged over from the minis-
ter's yard, a sole from grandfather's boot,
the wooden cover of a Webster's spelling
book, a cabbage stalk with roots deeply
entwined in a hunk of dirt, a mouldy corn-
cob, a rusty screw, and a good new clothes-
pin if nobody was looking.   We watched
the disappearance of these things in the
fire with great glee, and there was none of
the sober feeling that came over us when
the sticks and bait boxes went out of sight
in the flume.

A large part of the pond was spread with lilypads which shaded the reticulated pickerel, and round about the margins amphibious arrow-weeds lifted themselves up high enough to whisper to the companionable willows which leaned over the water as far as they dared, and which canopied the nest of the wood-thrush when she pressed her warm spotted breast over the satin-lined blue eggs that held hours and hours of coming song.

Twittering swallows slid in graceful curves over the surface of the pond, dipped their bills into the water as they flew, circled out over the hayfield and back to the pond again as lightly as mere allusive emblems of flight. Gaudy opercled sunfish built round nests in the yellow sand where the quawk waded with his phosphorescent breast lantern at night, and gauzy winged dragon-flies no heavier than mid-day air balanced upon the tippiest tips of the sedges. Archippus and argynnis butterflies drifted about over the clustered asclepias on the bank and the colias fleet luffed on the half-dried mud.

In the autumn the muskrats built cosy
houses of calamus and cattail at the
head of the pond, and one could find a
raccoon track under the button bushes if
he knew just where to pull the branches
aside to look for it. Wood-ducks floated
among fallen leaves in the shallow cove
where sere and brown grasses hung their
loads of rich nutritious seeds within easy
reach, and sometimes a black duck spent
two or three days among the frost-killed
weeds on the low islands where splashy
waves and autumn rains had made good
woodcock ground under the alders. Katy-
dids and tree crickets katydided in the
venerable and respected maple tree, while
the disbanded chorus of hylas piped with
solitary voices in the woods which had
been littered by a departing season. The
old rickety bridge lay slanting upon its
abutments. Its beams had been obliged
to yield a little in the spring freshet when
the ice had jammed against them. The
chestnut planking of the bridge was
warped, and where horses' feet had punc-
tured the rotting boards pine slabs were

nailed as a provision against accident and unwise expenditure. Hay seed that had sifted down from August loads sprouted in the dust on the girders, and it rattled down into the water when we turned up a plank in order to slyly poke a copper wire noose in front of the un-suspicious white-nosed suckers as they patiently worked from rock to rock along the bottom under the fancied protection of the bridge.

When winter came over the pond the hemlocks sighed very often, for they loved rivalry with other trees in foliage, and the blue jays went to them to offer sympathy. Green and blue added a bright bit of color to the white landscape and pursuaded the distant winter sky to come nearer. Soft-footed rabbits carelessly left whole rows of rabbit tracks in the snow where black-berry briers offered tempting nipping, and the thick rushes were as full of quail tracks as an egg is full of meat. In the cold, still winter midnight, when the be-lated traveller blew his frosted finger-tips and trudged noiselessly along through the fluffy snow in the lonely pond road, allowing superstition to keep one eye on the lookout, the muffled quunk, quunk, quunk, of uncaused ice sounds suddenly admonished him to take longer steps and to get some kind of a door behind him.

There was nothing mysterious about the pond in the daytime, and it was great fun to kick a stone out of the frozen ground and send it bounding across the ice ; to hear the musical whunk, whenk, whink, ink, inkle, inkle, inkle, inkle, until the stone bounced into the bushes on the further bank. How the ice did ring to the clipping skate strokes when we youngsters, red-mittened and with flying tippet ends, played shinny in the moonlight until the driftwood fire burned low and we realized that we had been out three hours later than the time when we had promised to be at home, where our good parents were consoling themselves with the thought that we always had come home previously. No matter how frosty the night, or how keenly the wind blew, we knew nothing of that while the fun

lasted, but it began to feel chilly when
Susie had chosen to go home with Dave,
and it became shivery when Ed had been
accepted as escort for Nellie. Pretty
brown-eyed Nellie with warm home-
knitted woollen stockings and glowing
cheeks, her mirthful eyes shining out
through a loosened lock of dark hair
under her fur-lined hood. We knew that
Ed would bashfully steal a cold-nosed,
hurried kiss at the gate, and that Nellie
would hit him with her skates, but not
very hard—not as hard as we would have
done it. We knew what would happen
because Ed had looked sheepish for a
whole week after he had gone home with
Nellie the last time, but we told each
other that we did n't care if Nellie did
like Ed the best. We did n't care a
darn bit, 'cos he wa'n't nobody nohow.
Could n't set rabbit twitch-ups, nor snare
suckers, nor play mibs for fair, and he only
knew 'rithmetic and school things. A
feller like that wa'n't no good and nobody
'ceptin' the teacher and Nellie liked him.
How little did we realize in those early

days that there was something green-eyed
as well as something brown-eyed out for
an outing when the weather was right;
but boys who are supposed to have no
troubles at all are all full of them, because
they have the emotions of older folks without the training to discover the locality
of a thorn. Many are their troubles which
make a lasting impression through life.

One of us boys was so enthusiastic
about trapping muskrats that he got up at
four o'clock every morning all through the
winter and tramped miles along the streams
before breakfast, watching the habits of
the warmer-coated denizens of the brook,
hunting for their holes under the banks
and the paths where they came up into
the meadow for grass. A heap of unio
shells had for him a meaning. A burrow
under the snow to a certain apple tree
showed which frozen apples the muskrats
liked best. A soggy, decayed log in the
water always carried a definite evidence
of their fondness for that spot, and the
boy knew that his trap would be sprung
and the sweet apple pulled from its stick

when he went to that log in the morning. The boy's interest and labor were well rewarded, and he caught more muskrats than any of the other boys who went to their traps when it was convenient and who did not set them in very good places anyway. It was a matter of so much pride to the boy to be successful that he told all of the other boys about his luck, and expected that they would pat him on the back and sing his praises as a famous hunter; but, ah! how much more had he learned about muskrats than about human nature. The other boys simply would not believe at first that he had such luck as he described, but he made them believe it by taking them out to the barn and showing them the skins carefully stretched upon shingles with flat tails all in a row. Did that end the difficulty? No indeed! The other boys straightway got ugly about it and said that if he had such luck as that he must have taken the muskrats out of their traps, and they told Nellie and Susie what they thought about it. Nellie and Susie responded with that

sympathy which is the sweetest of feminine characteristics, and promptly sided
with the injured ones. Such was the boy's
first experience in competing for gains ;
but in later life he found that whenever
perseverance and work made him successful over others who were less interested than he they at first refused to
believe, and when forced to believe decided that he must have employed unfair
means.

The boy was very much grieved at the
attitude of his companions, whose esteem
and good-fellowship were more to him
than the muskrat skins or the powder and
shot that they would buy. The problem
at one time seemed to end at nothing
short of his giving up the profitable trapping and letting the other boys do it all ;
but finally he hit upon the plan of telling
them of his best tricks, and showing them
the good trapping places that he had discovered at times when they were com-
fortably snoozing in bed. That eased the
strained relations somewhat, but as the
best luck, unfortunately, continued to pur-

lives a long way from the pond now, and his hair is grayer than it was in muskrat days, but it is a pleasure when visiting the old homestead to go over to the pond and hunt for the heaps of unio shells and the burrows under the bank, Ed and Nellie are married and have sons and daughters of their own, and he as a man of wide renown has proven that fraudulent estimates were furnished to us boys by the green-eyed dealer in the game of life. Dave and Susie drifted away from each other when Dave went off to college, and while his tastes were ascending, hers remained stationary, so that after a few years they were not companions for each other at all. She as a household drudge is very different from the happy Susie whose skates rang merrily with ours on the black ice under the winter stars. Joe and Pete, who failed to do much with the muskrats and who were ugly about it, have failed to get up early in any of their undertakings, and they often go for aid to the boy who tried to show them how to succeed in former days, but it is of no use. They still grum-

ble and complain of their lot, and are ever
ready to impugn the motives and the
methods of any man who is prosperous.
Jerry, who was about the dullest boy in
school, went West, and has made a fortune in railroads, so that it seems as though
almost anybody could do that ; but Henry,
who was one of the very best scholars, is
an extremely respectable clerk in Jerry's
employ, and he has never as yet perceived
opportunity standing out in as bold relief
as a fly in the milk. Tom was drowned
at sea, and no one seems to know what
has become of George. Everything has
changed excepting Hopkins's Pond, but
to-day the water pours over the dam as
of old, and the cricket's sharp chirp finds
its way through the duller sound. The
muskrat makes a rippling wake in the
moonlight, but I do not know whose boy
eagerly marks its course now. Pickerel
still suspend themselves under the lily-
pads, and a bullhead will pull any one's
cork 'way down under water on almost any
warm, misty evening. The pond that once
entered so much into the boys' life is now

entering into the lives of a new generation of boys.

One day recently Echo, up among the rocks, was heard protesting more loudly than · ever before, and soon a coaching party of sightseers with four bang-tailed horses and a brazen horn came rolling along the road. One of the ladies touched a gentleman on the arm and said, "There is a pond." The gentleman answered, "Yes." And the coach rolled on.

That was all that it meant to them, for they were sightseers.

BONASA UMBELLUS, REX.

KING by courtesy of all game birds and subject to no authority whatsoever is the proud ruffed grouse of our North American forest.

Named by Linnæus after the wild ox, *bonasus*, for his roaring, and specified as *umbellus* because of the arrangement of neck ornaments, he has received down through cyclefuls of generations a strength and beauty undegenerate. From the pines and hemlocks of the ravine he inhales the spirit and the energy of his moods. The wintergreens and birches furnishing provender, give spicy life to his nerves and muscles. From the crags he adopts the suggestion of ruggedness, and from the winter gale cons music for his symphony by wings. The crash of the falling dead tree involves an idea of death, and by opposites he rushes upward with startling roar to liberty and life when found by the hunter.

THE ROMANCE OF A GROUSE FAMILY.

Through a small south-facing valley in western New York there runs a spring trout brook. Several years ago the choppers cleared off the arm of woodland that extended from the main forest up along the stream, and then the swale was quite barren except for the crooked alders that had not been worth cutting, and for the fire-weeds that always come to the temporary assistance of newly cleared land.

Gradually the sheep and cattle began to find pasturage there, and two or three years later clumps of beech and poplar saplings sprang up. Patches of briers then crowded out the sparse grass, and here and there a thrifty green hemlock arose near the stump of its deposed ancestor, so that the barren ground that had become pasture land was transformed into a brush lot.

One Sunday morning in May the sun shone warmly in upon the budding saplings of the swale. The naiads of the brook murmured with hushed voices and the trailing arbutus which overhung the bank gave out a rarer fragrance than it would have done on any rude week day. Hardly a sound was heard save the wandering tones of the church bell in the far-off village, and the only appreciable motion of the air was in the gentle breaths that rise almost imperceptibly from the warming soil of quiet glades.

With almost noiseless footsteps a demure hen grouse walked from the edge of the thick moist woods and stopped for a moment a little way out in the brush lot. Again she went on and again paused, looked about her and listened, with one foot daintily lifted from the ground. Thus by degrees she advanced out among the saplings, her head gracefully moving back and forth in unison with her footsteps and the pretty brown neck feathers gliding so softly over each other that they seemed like one warp and woof of silk.

Stepping upon the gnarled root of a rough lichen-covered stump she glanced over her own smooth outlines and the bright hazel eye looked the satisfaction of the comparison, but yet she could not resist the feminine impulse to rearrange several feathers that were already perfectly in place.

All at once she gave a start, and with upstretched neck and elevated crest assumed an attitude of strictest attention, for from a distant point in the forest there had come to her ears a low sound like muffled drum-beats, the strokes first slow, then faster, and ending finally in a long tattoo.

Poised upon the root with partly opened wings, she seemed almost ready to fly in the direction from which the sound came, but suddenly remembering herself, the wings were closed again and her head dropped bashfully until the echoless drum-beat once more sounded through the woods. It was the love call of Old Ironsides, a noble cock grouse that we had so named because of his seeming impenetrability to the shot that had been fired at him time and again in the lower ravine where he chose to spend most of his time.   Day after day the hen grouse had listened for that call, knowing that Old Ironsides would come in the spring-time to find her.   And now should she fly impetuously to him and let him know her impatience at his delay?   Oh, no! The annals of feminine nature contain no history of such rash action, so taking an easy running jump into the air she flew very quietly among the trunks of the big trees of the woods, and then on curving wings sailed slowly near the ground to a point somewhere in his vicinity, and alighting, waited for further summons. The roll call sounded again, and she the only musterer walked half hesitatingly in the direction from which it came, sliding quietly as a mouse behind boulders and thick kalmia bushes, and looking as unconcerned as you please.

At last he was in sight.   High upon the prostrate trunk of a huge storm-riven pine he was pacing slowly to and fro with martial bearing, his proud crest raised, his broad tail partially spread, and all his feathers glinting in the lights of the woods.

The hen grouse was not many rods away, gliding stealthily from one hiding place to another, hoping that he would discover her and yet not daring to lose any of her reserve. How she did want to pull his black ruffs though, and strike him petulantly with her bill and pretend to be real angry at him for rough play!

For a moment Old Ironsides stopped his incessant pacing, glanced into the thicket on one side and on the other, and then his sturdy wings were struck repeatedly against his sides, sending forth the long vibrations of a tone so low that it seemed to roll along the ground rather than penetrate the upper air, but with such initial velocity, nevertheless, that it rolled half a mile out of the woods before losing itself in the grassy fields. How grand the old warrior looked to the hen grouse. But what if he should become impatient and fly elsewhere to seek her

and not return for a long week ?   No one
will ever know whether she purposely
stepped upon the small dead stick that
snapped and revealed her presence just
then, but who is prepared to deny a motive
for the seemingly accidental movement
of a dumb animal on such an occasion.

She was discovered and he was by her
side. Coyly she stepped away from him,
and then to gain further admiration,
which was all unnecessary, he spread his
great barred tail widely over his back, unfolded the iridescent black ruffs until they
concealed his shoulders, dropped his
curved wing-tips to the ground, elevated
his pointed crest, and with curved neck circled and pirouetted about her, nodding
his head, fixing his strong, bold eye upon
her modest one, and stepping in front of
her to head off retreat, in such an exas-
perating way that it seemed as though she
certainly would scream.

He would not have made any such pre-
tentious movements if other cock grouse
had been about to criticise him, and how
the other hen grouse would have been

amused at her assumption of simplicity
and gentleness. She who was the boldest
of all when associating with others of her
own sex, and who could roar as loudly
with her wings as any cock grouse when
trying to unnerve an enemy.

But who could doubt that all of this
display on his part meant that he was
assuring her that he would be, oh, so true
and loyal forever and forever? She believed in him most sincerely, and loving
and respecting tried hard to avoid being
annoyed at his overplus of attention.

It was not long afterward, however,
that he acted in a rather independent
manner and took little interest in family
affairs, so that when in June there was a
nest of ten eggs by the side of a clematis-
covered stump out at the edge of the
brush lot, Old Ironsides was either drum-
ming again in another woods altogether,
or he was associating with two or three
chummy reprobates of his own sex during
the livelong day.

The hen grouse took great comfort
with her eggs, though. Six of them were

plain buff-colored, and four of them were
marked with light-brown spots, and all
were smooth and snug-fitting in the nest.
Around about the nest she scratched some
dry, loose beech leaves which could be
whisked over the eggs in an instant with
one movement of her wings in event of
surprise by a marauder, and then, being
almost of the color of dead leaves herself,
she could hardly be seen when she snuggled cosily down over the eggs and drew
her head in closely.   It seems too bad to
think that after all this pains the mother
bird might be discovered in her hiding
place, alone and unprotected as she was.
One evening a red fox trotted past, and
when near the nest he stopped and sniffed
the air, twisting the sharp tip of his nose
from one side to the other, and alternately
spreading and closing his whiskers, but he
could not quite locate the gentle prey,
and his attention was finally attracted
elsewhere by a little squeaking evening
mouse that had fallen from the soft cedar
bark nest in the wild grapevine near by.

The noiseless swoop of a great ogre-

eyed horned-owl gave the mother grouse
a cruel heart-thumping one moonlight
night just as she had almost dared to take
a little nap ; but the owl had dived for a
gray. rabbit, and did not suspect that a
grouse was within easy reach.   Why it
was that the minks and skunks and
weasels and raccoons and box turtles and
black snakes did not find the nest is a
mystery ; but there is some strange protection afforded by nature for ground-
nesting birds.   Perhaps there is a certain
sense of honor among predaceous animals.
Hounds are disinclined to chase a nursing
she-fox, and it may be that minks know
better than to destroy the eggs that make
the golden geese, although we do know
that they are sometimes absent-minded in
their morals.   The only enemy that found
the nest after all was a farmer's boy, and
he did it quite accidently by stepping so
near the old bird. on his way home from
the trout brook that she was forced to fly
out.   The boy's first impulse was to leave
the eggs undisturbed except for the turning that was absolutely necessary for an

accurate count, but suddenly remembering that there was a "settin' hen" under
the old wagon in the woodshed at home,
he smiled a salute of thanks to his memory, and with well-meaning but rather
thick-fingered caution that would have
made most of us a little nervous if they
had been our eggs, he rolled up two of
the precious oval treasures in a youthful
fisherman's Saturday afternoon handker-
chief, and tucking them carefully away in
a side pocket trudged rather unsteadily
over the stones as his mind became occupied with the thought of having two live
grouse at home that would respond to his
kindly efforts to tame them.   At intervals
he regretted that he had not taken two
more of the eggs ; but his conscience was
quieter at knowing that the mother bird
could bear two pangs more easily than
four when she returned to the nest again.

For eighteen long days the mother
grouse had been sitting, and she anxiously
awaited the welcome sound of a little one
tapping at the shell for release.   While
she had been waiting the blood-roots and

dog-tooth violets had dropped their petals, the white cornel flowers had turned to a feeble fading pink, the hepaticas and anemones become dingy, and in their places the azaleas and trilliums came out in full sponsal array. The ferns, which fought their way through the resisting cold ground with clenched fists, had now unfolded a generous wealth of fronds under the influence of a spring-time sun which brought harmony for all nature with its presence.

The patient bird had seen the hosts of warblers proceed bush by bush and tree by tree from the southland toward the northland, and it was time for her brood to appear. When at last she heard a faint tip-tapping and saw a movement through a long crack in one egg, it was not long before the gentle aid of her bill had released a cunning little yellow and brown head. Then a small struggling wing appeared, and out tumbled a dear, downy chick of a grouse. One after another the eight young birds escaped, and one of them in his hurry to be in the world with us ran around as soon as his legs protruded; and comical enough he looked with the broken shell clinging to his back.

At about this time the old Brahma hen over at the farmhouse found under her feathers two chickens that were smaller than any that she had ever seen before, and they were ahead of any calculations that she may have made as to time; but she felt fully responsible for them, nevertheless, and was disturbed because they ran away from her sheltering wings and only returned to her most persistent clucking. The boy, who had been attracted by the solicitous calls of the hen, caught one of the agile scampering balls of down in his hand and held it up to admire the bright eyes and tiny bill that were thrust through between his fingers; but the little feet clutched his fingers so tightly, and the small heart throbbed so fast, that in pity he put the grouse chicken quickly down by the old Brahma hen again. What transformation a little warmth had wrought in the cold senseless yolk and white of the egg of a few days before, changing it into a beautiful warm little creature endowed with hopes, and fears, and longings, and knowing its friends from its enemies.

But what strange instinct was it that kept leading these two babes of the wood away from the motherly barnyard hen? What did they seek so persistently? Scarce an hour had elapsed since their escape from the shell, and they had wandered out of hearing of the good foster mother to seek a wild mother who would train their wild little natures in full sympathy and understanding. Down into the garden they ran, then out across the lane and into the grass in the meadow. Whither they were going they knew not, but go they must. They were hungry, but there was no mother to teach them to eat, and thirsty without knowing what water was. All day long they ran through the grass and under the rail fences—first brother ahead, then sister—the strange impulse urging their tiny pattering feet ahead as fast as they could go. It

was chilly in the evening and their soft
down was all wet and bedraggled with
dew, and when it became too dark for
them to see the way, they stopped by a
sheltering stone and snuggled up close to
each other with plaintive peeps ; but they
were too tired to sleep and every now and
then the drooping eyelids opened with a
start and the chicks pushed closer still to
each other and lisped their longings for a
mother's warm feathers.   On the following morning they could not run nearly so
fast, and very often they stumbled and
fell over the sticks and weed stalks that
seemed to them to offer more and more
opposition.   The pretty down was rough-
ened so that it stuck together every which
way, and all forlorn they were indeed.   If
one lagged far behind or chirped patheti-
cally when caught in a tangle of grass the
other would toddle back and wait, for
even such mites of birds felt the desire
for companionship in misery.   Every few
minutes they had to stop and rest, and
again on they would struggle, but with
such weak, uncertain steps that it was

evident that their trifling energies were
almost expended long before the cold dew
had again soaked and chilled them.   They
were not so very far from the brush lot
where their real mother was, but that night
when the two tender little wanderers tried
to comfort each other there was not a bit
of warmth for them to exchange and they
shivered and trembled so that they could
not have kept very close together anyway.
The morning sun·looked down upon two
wee wet grouse babies lying side by side
in the field.   Their eyes were closed,
their yearnings had all ceased, and no one
would have distinguished them from the
quartz stones of the field.   Such a short
experience with life !

All of this while the mother grouse was
having care enough with her brood of
eight, even if two were missing.   They
would eat nothing but insects, and it kept
the old bird pretty busy scratching over
the leaves to find enough for them.   In
one corner of the brush lot there was a
large red-ants' nest, and there the chickens
had great fun when they had grown to

be nimble of foot. The mother would scratch away a part of the loose heap of soil, and then when the ants bustled out, some devoted to angry passions and others hurrying to carry off the long white eggs that had been exposed, the little chickens became so expert at snapping them up that in the conceit born of successful experience they even chased a fly in the absurd expectation of catching it, and the fly was so much surprised at their assurance that it allowed itself to be caught, for such is often the relation of ambition to seeming impossibilities. One needs only to be stupid enough to obtain everything.

The young birds grew rapidly and became experts at avoiding their natural enemies. If a sharp-shinned hawk flew over, the mother gave a warning note, and instantly each chick dropped so flat against the ground that it was impossible for the very best eyes to see one of them. When the farmer's boy again had occasion to cross the brush lot the hen bird had advised the chickens to hide long before

3

he came near them, for even if he had
not cared to disturb the little ones, such a
boy may accidentally tread directly upon
angels if he does not see them, and to
lead him away the mother fluttered and
limped along the ground, pretending to be
lame and unable to fly. The boy knew
well this trick of the bird, but she pre-
tended to be so really in distress this time
that he floundered after her through the
briers. When he was far enough away,
however, she took to her wings as usual,
and circled by a long route back to the
brood again. One cluck was sufficient to
cause the ground to spring into life about
her, and the chickens were all safe.

A hooded adder that was sunning himself in the dry sheep-path one day suddenly awoke and found a chicken quite near
him, and although the little thing was too
much frightened to run very fast it nevertheless got out of the dangerous vicinity
in time, and the adder had to console himself with a fat cricket. What luck for the
chicken that it was a slow adder instead
of a black racer, for the latter would have

followed it at any necessary rate of speed, and after mesmerizing it by the cruel charming of cross glides and super-ambient head and fulgurating tongue, would finally have ended the vicious play by creeping an ugly gullet over the soft prey.

There was one enemy, though, that came so insidiously that the mother gave no warning note, and it would have availed nothing if she had done so. A great harmless blue heron had just sagged along over the brook in awkward flight, when from his wake came a winged tick, the dreadful lipoptena, buzzing in eccentric lines until he espied the grouse. With devilish precision of aim the uncanny harpy of a thing struck the soft feathers of her back and disappeared among them with an eerie sidewise glide. The very thought of harboring such a parasite was enough to make the grouse shudder, but she feared more for the little ones than for herself. Follow the tick as she would with her bill when a wriggling feather disclosed its locality she could not find the horrible thing, until at evening, when the chicks were gathered about her it huskily buzzed from her breast. She caught it quickly, but could not swallow it for the tough elastic legs had encircled the edge of her bill, nor could she crush it because the leathery body expanded in any direction when she brought all her strength to bear upon it. Finally the foul tick in the most unconcerned manner deliberately crawled from her bill and with its fiendish directness struck the neck of one of the handsomest of the brood and fastened itself there firmly in the intention of remaining in spite of all remonstrance. On the following day the tick, swelling with the life blood of the chicken, discarded its wings as an evidence of determination to remain, and a few days later it gave birth to a single offspring, full-winged and ready for attack. The young imp fastened itself to the chicken's neck close by its parent, and no matter how hard the mother grouse pulled at them she only succeeded in stretching out their rubber-like bodies and in pulling her little chick off from his feet. Day by

day the poor chick grew thinner and
scrawnier, while his sturdy brothers and
sisters went steadily along in development,
and the brood would soon have numbered
only seven had not the mother bird fortu-
nately led them far into the dank, cool
swamp on one torrid day, where much to
their delight was found a patch of skunk
cabbage with its heavy fruit.   How the
mother did enjoy tearing open the green
fleshy balls for the seeds, and the little
fellows feasted upon the pulp like veritable
gluttons, not knowing that at the same
time the life of the invalid in their family
was to be saved.   The pungent aroma
had only just begun to circulate through
their veins when the young tick loosed his
death-like grip and buzzed from one
chicken to another, trying to find one that
was agreeable, but they were all alike and
so it sidled up to a passing rabbit and
there found lodgment.   In a few days it
had discarded its wings and then there
was no danger of its troubling the young
grouse again.   The old tick had tumbled
off overpowered at the same time that the

young one flew, and that night she was picked up on the sticky end of a toad's long tongue and successfully swallowed. Glory be to the toad !

In July the chickens began to feast upon huckleberries, and when the August black-berries were ripe they ate so many and grew so fast that it soon became time for them to throw off their short suits of soft brownish chicken feathers and to take on the finer colors and stout quills of real grouse.   With their change in dress came a change in tastes, so that they no longer cared for insects, but sought instead the ripened seeds and berries and tender leaves, unconscious of the fact that the shooting season was near at hand and that such diet was making them perilously fat and luscious.

As their wings became stronger and their tails grew longer, pride began to ap-pear in different members of the family and quarrels were frequent among the youngsters.   They were disobedient, and stayed away from home at night when-ever it pleased them to do so.   The mother grouse was not much disturbed at this demonstration of independence, for she knew that she had raised a brood of the wildest birds of the forest, and now in September she was willing to leave them to their own resources, satisfied that she had trained them all properly in ways of self-protection.

THE AUTOCRAT OF THE EDDY.

GRAPEVINES and moonseeds and Virginia creepers tangle their branches together over the prostrate form of the old lichen-covered mill. The thump and rumble of the soggy wheel have not been heard in the quiet little valley for many a year, and the water splashes over the drippy alga-decked shaft and through the holes in the dam, throwing clouds of cooling spray into the warm sunshine.

Collecting its scattered forces the stream bounds off among the rocks, slides under the ferns, and tarries for an eddy at the bend where the scraggy hemlock leans, giving the flecks of foam time to circle about in the shade before they are whirled away down stream again.

Deeply sunken beneath the hemlock's gnarled root is a shelving drift boulder of gneiss, and under the shelf a big trout has lived for many seasons. His colors are dark, his protruding under-jaw is hooked, his eye is fierce, and his manner is aggressive. No other living thing of his size or less would dare claim a share of the eddy. The beautiful despot has caught every baby trout that ventured so far up or down stream this year, and rumor has it that he swallowed one of his best children at a single gulp. The timid little dace hide behind the stones in shallow water and make eyes at him, but one by one he takes them to his bosom and shows them the folly of their ways. When a miller balances on the tip of a waving fern frond near the brink, the old trout throws water at it with his tail and then whirls it under, leaving a single white wing to float off down stream and make the other trouts mouths water. That shows his disposition.

The hemlock has stood on the bank for a couple of centuries and the trout has lived under it for a decade, but I have no dates for the boulder and the stream.

When the winter storm fills the branches with snow and cold winds moan as they roam through the forest, the eddy is covered with ice, but down at the edge of the boulder the big trout tucks the dark water snugly about him, slowly waves his broad tail back and forth, passes an occasional glassful of water through his gills, and cares nothing for the storm and the cold, but in quiet contemplation looks forward with pleasure to the sins of a new season.   If the little white-footed mouse hops trembling across the ice, the trout is sorry he cannot take her down into his comfortable home, but there is a coldness between the trout and the mouse that he loves, and little does the mouse suspect that the bump which she felt on the ice under her feet was made by the nose of one that would fain approach nearer.

When the birds come back in the spring and the blue-bird, nestling in the sunny top of the hemlock, softly carols a love song about Bermuda, the black and white

warbler breaks the brown monotony of
the rough bark as he glides up, down and
around it, and the aromatic fragrance of
the hemlock mingles with the gentler odor
of red maples and anemones and new
moss, the trout still spends his days near
the shelf of the boulder and watches for
the flies that the phœbe bird misses.
When he plunges out after them the timid
rabbit hops convulsively backward and
opens his great wondering eyes more
widely than ever, and the red squirrel
scurries up the hemlock trunk, scolding
and jerking his tail to give emphasis to
his remarks; but nothing can the rabbit
and the squirrel see except a few circling
ripples chasing each other ashore.

When the summer days come, the
cicada sounds his shrill call from the dead
limb overhead, the noise of clinking
scythes is borne from the hay-field to the
woods, and the hot breath of the brakes
almost smothers the asters on the bank as
they look longingly at their cool reflec-
tions in the brook. The surroundings
have changed, but the trout lies deep

down in his favorite place. If a cow wades into the eddy for a drink he does not care. If a clap of thunder makes the ground tremble, he is only a little bit uneasy; but there is one sound that puts him on the alert for danger. He does not often hear a fisherman's step, it is true, but he associates a few startling events with that sound. The stony New England soil cannot compete with the fertile Western lands; the farmers' boys have gone off to the cities, and the few elderly people who remain care a good deal more for 'lection and meetin' than they do for fishing. But sometimes persons who were once boys go back to the old homesteads during the hot summer days, and these old boys have not forgotten the brook nor the trout that they used to string on a forked willow stick, as slippery as it was yellow. The big trout has not had experience with so very many hooks, but perhaps once a year for the last ten years he has had a misunderstanding with a fisherman, and ten lasting impressions have been made on his memory.

For eleven months and one week in every year the hemlock, the boulder, the eddy, and the trout are inseparable ; but when in the late September days the squealing wood-duck paddles among the floating dead leaves with his pretty red feet, and the muskrat with thickening fur dives under the boulder in search of a winter home, the trout has departed.

Then it is that one can hear inquiring voices among the brook sounds if he will sit quietly and not disturb the nymphs. Under the hemlock's roots the voices are low and congratulatory.   The nymphs there know the old rascal too well to wish him back again, but they seem afraid to speak much above a whisper, and they hardly dare inquire for news among their neighbors in the rocks ; but every now and then a sprightly voice from up stream or from down stream will call impatiently for an answer from the eddy.   An upstream sprite asks if a mink has caught the trout, and softly comes an answer, saying that the trout has learned by experience to lie so near the bottom that a mink cannot seize him from below, and he certainly could not be caught fairly. " How about the water snakes?" asks another; and the reply, " He is too large for them to fight," comes back in a moment. " Has a snapping-turtle caught him?" is asked; but a dozen replies at once say that no snapping-turtle has passed along the stream for a year and a half. " Has a fisherman got him?" asks one; and such a chuckling and laughing comes from all sides that one is quickly convinced that the fisherman is the least dangerous of the four enemies of the trout.

The fact of the matter is that in the fall the old trout's fancy lightly turns to thoughts of love, and in this connection I might as well say that of late years he has been guilty of bigamy. Formerly he would quietly leave the eddy on a late September day, and go down stream to a shallow nook where a lively spring made the sand boil up at the bottom in four or five puffs at a time; where the caddis worms built their armor of sticks and mica scales, and where alders growing thickly, arched their branches overhead and shaded the pool.   In this bower he found his lovely wife patiently waiting for him, and although he would pay her pretty close attention for a few days and pretend to be interested, he would soon wander about and flirt with the little girl trout, who went wild over his beauty but who had never seen the old villain at home in his eddy.

Two or three years ago, however, a heavy ice floe coming down in the spring freshet knocked a new hole in the dam, and whenever the water is high enough in early October, the trout runs up through the hole, and goes to see a wife that he met under the lily-pads in still water in the pond.   She is larger even than he is, and lazier, and not nearly so attractive as the down-stream wife.   Her eggs too are dull yellow, while the down-stream wife's eggs are bright straw color, and why it is that he enjoys the pond trout's company no one can tell; but there's no accounting for tastes.

The old trout is not very deeply affected

by love, and he is always back at the
boulder by the middle of October.

Just a word about his children's nursery :

Down where the sunshine is stirred in the water
  By zephyrs that bend the thin tops of the sedge,
The stream shallows out at the head of the meadow,
  And dammed by a log, widens more at the edge.

The nettles are rank on the rich bank about it,
  And out on the log straggle tussocks of grass ;
Beneath the warm driftwood the cricket is chirping,
  And green-headed frogs tune their throats for
    the class.

The little trout practise at vaulting and leaping,
  And stir up the sand in their still, shallow pool ;
From daylight to darkness, and all through the
    moonlight,
  They try every trick that is taught in their school.

They strain at a gnat and then swallow a lady-bug ;
  Deep into air they all dive for a fly ;
But larger they're growing, not learning the lesson
  That careless ones jumping at feathers may die.

And some of them reaching the age of discretion,
  Will solemnly hunt for a deep shady hole ;
And like their old father—as cruel as Nero—
  Will live as they please, without conscience or
    soul.

I wonder if the old trout remembers my attempt at getting him out upon the bank last June. Cautiously I had crept to a point where the bushes hid me from sight, and slid the tip of the slender split-bamboo rod through the same opening through which the alder pole had been poked so many times in years gone by. With a slight cast, the brown-hackle and coach-man and Reub Wood were tossed over the lair of the trout, and drawn in enticing zig-zags between the foam flecks on the water. It was not the first time that arti-ficial flies had failed to tempt him, and when the cast was changed to a grizzly-king, a silver-doctor, and a stone-fly, he just kept perfectly still, and let me go through all the motions of fishing, as though that were all I had gone out for.

Under a fungus-covered log I found a handsome pink and squirming angleworm, that did its very best on a bait hook deep down where the trout's nose ought to have been, but there was no demonstra-tion of appreciation on the part of the

4

autocrat of the eddy.   Next I found in
the moss a crimson newt that looked
delicious enough for anybody to bite, and
when the hook was carefully passed
through a small fold of skin, so as not to
hurt much, he was tossed over into the
pool.   Around and around in little circles
the newt swam, and deeper and deeper,
until there was only a faint red wriggle to
be seen way down by the shelf of the
rock.   Suddenly a vigorous tug whisked
the tip of the rod under water, the reel
gave a scream, and then all was quiet
again ; but I could feel the old fellow's
teeth grating on the tense line as he sul-
lenly moved his head from side to side.
Every instant I expected a rush up stream,
and a tumbling wrestle in the swift water
above the eddy, but still there was ominous quiet.   There I stood all ready for
action, the tip of the rod curved over and
almost dipping into the water, the line
drawn as tightly as a banjo string and
leading straight down into the depths of
the slow current.   Gradually reeling in
the line, the trout came heavily to the sur-

face with all fins set, and surging doggedly back and forth with short strokes of his sturdy tail.

What could such tactics mean? Why was he reserving his strength at a moment when, according to my notion, he ought to be tearing about in frantic efforts to escape? The landing-net was reached out toward him. It was almost under him when, with a tremendous plunge, he threw a shower of spray in my face, and the broken line, swishing through the air, snarled among the hemlock branches high up out of reach.

The hook has worked out of his mouth by this time, and at this very moment he lies at the edge of the boulder beneath the hemlock, waving his tail slowly to keep his position in the uncertain current of the eddy. When the stream roars with autumn rains he will swing his tail to the rhythm of the roar. When it thunders in the spring freshet he will churn the strong current with defiant tail strokes, and stay by his boulder. When the summer stream is gentle he will wave his tail softly near the bottom sands, and poise by the shelf of gneiss; and as years go on there will still be found together the hemlock, the boulder, the eddy, and the trout.

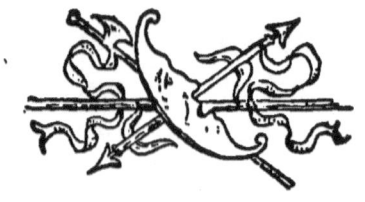

WATCHING THE BRANT
GROW BIG.

THE raw east wind is shiver-laden.
Fine grains of sand scurrying along
the frozen beach rattle into the ghastly
open mouth and out through the ragged
bones of the breeze-dried gurnard. A
song-sparrow flips for a moment into a
thrummed marsh elder and then falls into
the salty desiccated grass again and hides
himself away from a wind that askews his
tail and parts his soft feathers almost to
the place where his cheery song is concealed. It is not time for him. He
helps make springtime but cannot do it
all alone. Wait, little one, we give you
credit. A herring-gull essays to give life
to the March morning by hovering in low
circles over the ruffling black channel
water, and then finds it more in keeping

to stop and merge his color into that of a stranded ice floe in the distance. The leaden heaven moves slowly over us, unbroken save for the slanting missiles of sleet that peck against the cabin window and then bound full tilt to their grandmother the good old South Bay. Captain Jack, finishing his early cup of hot coffee down below, comes up out of the companion-way on deck in his woollen shirt, hitches up one suspender, runs his hands through his grizzly unwilling hair, hawks and expectorates over the rail. "Golly! Tide runs like a hoss, don't it?" says he, as a tangle of submerged eel-grass scratches alongside in the swift ebb, and the bowsprit of the sloop sidling in the inlet current, bunts a periwinkle shell out of the hard marsh bank that protected us at anchor during the night. Captain Jack does not produce much effect in the landscape about the marshes, because he looks so much like any natural object—excepting when he comes to town. He has stout muscles and a good heart. 'T is only his head that fails when he comes in contact with civilization.

The sea air smells. It is growing richer with the exhalations from looming flats as the tide shrinks, and with ozone from the growling, muttering surf of the outer beach. I, eagerly inhaling, find in distending lungfuls of it the peace of the infusoria of the flats and the power of the grand, swinging ocean. Every breath soiled by me is carried onward and away to the westward and replaced by a new one. How long, clean east wind, before I am translucent within? For last night we left the city where men call air the emanations from percolating swill and cast-off things, and where the tarnishing atmosphere, laden with entities of death, reeks in the nostrils and dulls the eyes of that poor mammal whose brain hangs dependent over figures and fads, amid the walls and corridors and walls again, that keep from him the sight of this sweet world. Is any other love like love for nature? Is any joy like the joy of the sportsman? I have seen the mother with eyes suffused with tears of love for the chubby boy in her arms. I have heard the maiden pray for power to love her lover more. But these loves are uncertain. The boy grows wicked and brings gray hairs and tears of sorrow. The lover is better pleased with another. But nature is steadfast. In the city the slinking street-cur brings forth her mongrel whelps beneath the wharf, not knowing whence shall come the food to turn to milk, and the pampered pug, bonbon-fed, has not the strength to propagate her kind. But here all life multiplies, and in abundance, and forever.

The bars of sand that divide currents into currents and that direct the apportionment of bay waters, are shining yellow here and there, and the white froth rolls up and blows across them. Hark ! From out the west a merry, flying rabble appears, buffeting the winds, caring naught for the cold. A rabble of warm birds that on even line head down the bay with hurrying wings and outstretched necks, chanting as they go, and in good company. Hark to the sound of their voices as they pass. Did ever crowd of students seem more hilarious ? Did ever more careless throng play easy with the elements ? One sings, and then another. Hear then all throats together. Here a cluck and there a tremolo, then back and forth the slogan goes till the disappearing huddle leaves in its wake vibrations that have softened the winds and set the waves to tune. To-night when all is still in the cabin you may hear those voices of the morning when no birds are near. When you are at home in the city, a strange, weird music will come as you sit before the grate fire in the twilight. The chimney winds have caught the cadence of the voices of the brant, and looking into the gloom of the room you will see again the moving wings that float adown the ceiling. 'T is the shadow of vibrations that have come from the far-off bay. No others can hear the sound or see the motion. 'T is for you alone, this delight of wandering impression that comes through miles of shadow, to you sympathetic.

Upon a narrow sand-bar lapped oy the receding waves, Captain Jack and I step out, to be saluted by the jets of forty clams. We will not forget this recognition on their part when it is time to return to the boat. In the sand-bar there is a sunken box just big enough for me to hide in. Its edges are level with the surface of the sand, excepting where the last high tide wanted some of the sand to make little wavy ridges with. Captain spades up fresh sand to hide the box with, and while this is being done I walk to a higher part of the bar that has not been under water for three or four tides. The wind has thrown the light sand into waves and ridges, just as the water would have done it. So wind and water are good chums off on the Bay. Here is a bunch of old wrack that pulled a scallop shell from its quiet bed, and came to grief on the bar. Here is a dried bit of leathery devil's apron that was torn from an ocean meadow perhaps by some derelict hull roving in the faintly-lighted depths without commission. Here is a cork that once was young and tender bark in Spain, growing under southern stars until men bargained for it with money. Then it perhaps saw one carousal after travelling to foreign shores, and it will be buried on this cold bar by shifting sands. Here is a feather that was shaken from the wing of a goose yesterday, when I was not as near as this to the goose. All about in the sand are tracks of plebeian gulls, but here is something better—here is the patrician track made by the pretty black foot of a brant.

I lie down flat upon my back in the box. The brant decoys are standing all about so naturally that only the Captain and I would suspect them to be such false things. I am waiting. The box is cold and wet. The spray flies into my eyes. The surf roars in the distance. One eye peers over the edge of the box and scans the horizon. What a jingle of wings was that, as a beautiful whistler and his homely mate passed overhead. They have finished the preliminary love experience early in the year, and are now constant and true to each other long before the spring zephyrs have felted into love the vagarious fancies of other water fowl. How strange that the male should be the most beautiful among almost all living things excepting the people. And yet the male whistler, superb as he is, had to seek his mate and go through a lot of nonsense, just as though she were a beautiful girl.

I did not shoot at that pair of whistlers. They would have made an excellent stew, with pork and potatoes in the same pot ; but they were so happy with each other that I allowed them to pass. It makes my mouth water now to think of them for dinner, but the treason is all in my stomach and not a bit of it in my heart. Flocks of brant are moving down the bay in straggling bunches or in even lines. Some oysterman has stirred them up, or perhaps they think that the eel-grass is more tender farther on, and they will en- joy it until it seems to be not quite so good as the grass that they left. Few people know why the brant move back and forth in this way, but I know just how they feel, because I have many times camped on one end of a pond and always found the fishing best away up at the other end, no matter which end I camped on. Thus the eel-grass in the distance is always green for the brant.

Four brant are coming this way. Are they coming this way or will they choose some other bar? They are winnowing along low over the water and apparently looking for companions. I throw up one foot to attract their attention. They see it. They slacken speed and "lift" for a better view. Yes! They see the decoys. Look out now! On they come and bigger they grow. At first they were no larger than pigeons, now they are as big as ducks, and in a moment more they will look as big as rocs, before my very eyes, and right here with me—all of us active—in a few cubic feet of the world. They have ability to be elsewhere, but they won't use their resources in time. They will be right here in the midst of the trouble. They call to the decoys. I answer. How fine and black their shapely heads and necks. What strong brown wings. They are coming. Now they swerve to the northward. There they circle back, showing white flanks as they wheel into line. They are not coming. They are going toward the middle of the bay. See that persistent one. He wants to come to me and the others do not, but that one is so determined that the others weaken in their good judgment and follow him. Now they stop fluttering. One sets his wings, another sets his wings, all four set their wings, and come slantting down an easy incline of air right toward the decoys. Neck and neck, wing and wing, tail and tail, on they come. Up I jump and breed confusion. "*Ronk!*" says one, and down through the smoke he tumbles with a mighty splash. "*Kruk! Kruk!*" says another, and then he makes the spray fly ten feet into the air at the edge of the bar, and causes the clams to squirt for rods around. "*B-r-a-n-t! B-r-r-r-a-n-t! B-r-r-r-a-n-t!*" say the other two, swishing themselves right up into high air. Yes, brant they are, and beauties too.

The March wind is piercing, the box is damp, the flying sleet rattles on my coat. I lie upon my back listening to the lapping of the waves, the crepitation of shifting sand, the rustle of the moving tide and the voices of distant brant and gulls. The cold clouds overhead have no comfort in them. My teeth chatter and a tear runs down my right cheek. Wet sand sticks to the skin between my red fingers. One small mouthful of just the right thing suffices to start in my innermost depths a dull cherry red glow that gradually diffuses itself in grateful warmth to the middle of every bone and to the ends of my wet sandy fingers. Who would object to that, I'd like to know? Now then for another brant. There comes one from away up the bay. Is he going or coming? Coming! No—going! Well, it all depends on which end his head is placed, and I cannot tell from here. He is coming! Bigger he grows and rounder he appears, and being alone will seek company. He sees the decoys and comes straight toward them without regard to the direction of the wind. Now he stops flying and comes tilting along unsteadily on curved set wings, balancing, sidling, balancing, coming, growing bigger and bigger as he skims the foamy, splattering waves without quite touching them. I'll let him alight. There, now! Right on the bar between me and the decoys. How trim his outlines are, and how gracefully he walks for one of the goose family. Why do those bright dark eyes fail to perceive me? He is young, as his wing coverts show by their ashy tipped feathers, and knowing that age is to be respected he puts confidence in the old decoys, unwilling to believe that I am terrible. He scoops up a billful of sand here and there where it looks particularly tempting, and asks the decoys something in a low voice. Now, I must take him into the box, for other brant will be coming. He jumps almost like a woodcock as I show him a great jack-in-a-box, and—Halloa! Right barrel snapped; left one shot a little under as the wind slanted him to one side. There he goes as fast as ever he can, away, away, away. I never saw that brant before in all my life and never shall see him again.

Out of the west horizon a corps of

twenty brant comes marching along
through the air, as orderly as soldiers.
I throw up a hand to attract their attention. They swerve. They wanted to
come to this bar in the first place, but
they have somewhere seen someone else
throw up a hand to them, and the old
ganders are suspicious. There are too
many eyes in that flock. Some of the
younger birds start toward the bar again
and the wary ones follow. Good judgment does n't count among friends. On
they come with a great clamor, some rising, some settling, some hoarse, some
clear voiced, some curving their wings to
sail in, some fluttering and wavering and
giving cries of warning. The whole flock
huddles and separates, and huddles and
rises, and wheels to go away. Then they
turn and head for the decoys again, but
the old birds have mounted high enough
to peer over into my box and they cry
" Look ! Look !" with such vigor that the
whole drove again whirls into a broadside
for final departure nearly twenty rods
away. The shot slaps and cracks against

their feathers, but only one bird slips out of the flock and drops perpendicularly into the water, while the rest choose a horizontal trajectory. Too many eyes. Too far away.

It is almost noon. The tide has fallen so far away that there is no water near the bar, and no more birds will come until another tide has risen. There is plenty of humble game within reach for the larder, though. Razor clams first! The edges of their shells are just on a level with the soft sand of the flat, but they must be approached gently, for they are sensitive in the company of strangers, and the fingers of a hungry enemy will grasp only a little maelstrom of roily water unless he is careful. I seize one of the razors, but how hard he pulls! Working him back and forth rapidly in his hole causes the water to loosen the sand all about him, and up comes a long, fat fellow, twisting his white foot in efforts to escape. When we work a razor back and forth in his hole the sand around him becomes mushy, according to a definite plan of nature, which turns the chances immediately against the clam in favor of the one who ought to have him. It will not do to be greedy and pull too quickly, for nature has decreed that in such case the microbes are to have the plump separated foot, while man is to content himself with the pretty shell containing only liver and gills and other organic bric-a-brac. It does not take long to gather a handful of razor clams, but that is not enough, and I cannot lay them down while gathering more because they would walk off and poke themselves endwise into the sand while I was looking the other way. It makes one feel like a cannibal to eat such lively animals, but if men are half as sweet as razor clams, we must be cautious about criticising the habits of the Sandwich Islanders of the old school. I cannot lay this handful down, so my cap must answer for a basket. A fine panful of razors we finally have on the deck of the sloop. Capt. Jack sets up serried ranks of them in the dripping-pan and puts small pieces of bacon in odd nooks and corners. When they are done a delicious steaming morsel lies upon a gaping shell, all ready for a little lump of butter and a plunge for the good of those chosen ones who know how to catch razor clams.

We pull the boat up out of the main channel and spear a few eels. Over miles of this bottom one can strike a spear blindly into the mud with fair probability of hitting an eel that has stored himself up for the winter a few inches below the surface, and in choice spots two eels sometimes come up at once on the tines of the spear. It is taking unfair advantage to spear the half-torpid things, but they are delectable and that makes a difference. Then again we can get revenge on behalf of the crabs, for nothing is more relentless than an eel that has set out to remove one by one the legs of a confused and most uncomfortable soft crab. We can spare the denizens of the bottom many such sights by incarcerating a bucketful of the offenders. When there are eels enough in the pail we push the boat over quahog ground, and no matter how hard it blows or how fiercely the sleet drives, a lot of round quahogs are soon rolling into the scuppers and wedging themselves into the rake just as our fingers get warm and dry. We have to be a little cautious in walking about, because it is a well-known fact that the quahog will turn when trodden upon.

Now for the soft-shelled clams that fired a salute when we alighted upon their bar in the morning. The shooting-box spade turns them out of their compact moulds in the sand half a dozen at a time. Tender and luscious they are, and so corpulent that they cannot draw their necks into the shell and close the shell at the same time. Just one thing more and the larder is complete for the day. We anchor in deep water between the submerged flats and crack open a quahog, putting a sweet clean piece upon the hook, and casting the line astern. In a minute the sinker is dancing; I give a quick jerk and then . bring up hand over fist a fish as flat as a flounder and weighing about a pound, made of just the right shape to fit the bottom of a frying-pan and become nicely browned on both sides when the fins curl up in a crisp. Five or six flappy flounders are pulled up on deck, and away we go again to our safe anchorage. Who would ever go hungry on the Great South Bay? There, within a radius of half a mile, we have helped ourselves abundantly to brant, razor clams, quahogs, soft clams, eels and flounders, and have had such fun in doing it that we want the man who is prepared for suicide to come down here for one day's sport before he decides that life is really too much of a bother. Our hands are cold, our clothes are wet, especially at vital points. Our noses and ears would do yeoman service in a summer refrigerator. But the cabin stove has a red hot lid, and the change to dry warm woollen clothing with a cup of hot coffee will pay for a month of discomfort. I am sorry for the man who never stops to think how well off he is with his every-day clothes on.

THE LAIR OF SOMETHING STRIPED.

THAT rock 's awash, aswash. Tighter draws the mussel on his byssus. The tide has turned. A thousand kelp streamers point the way the flood must go, and eagerly, not drooping as at last of ebb when obedience had seemed to satisfy their importuning.

The seeping barnacles make merry and clap their valves, for diatoms are coming, the sweet, the beautiful, food for the rough and ugly; coming from the devious gardens that they glorified among the schist splinters and boulders, beneath the swelling and subsiding and unceasing flow of green illumined sea water.

The rock is yet uncovered. No 't is not. And then once more it seems to sink, till the lolling pelage of wrack lifts

up a sign for help to the slow sweep of an
engulfing wave, and welters disconsolate
though the saved rock again appears. It
is not to disappear for long, this archaic
boulder of granite. It has never moved
but once e'en though the mammoth rubbed
it with his woolly ear or the heedless elas-
mosaurus bounced against it in the chase.
It moved but once, and then the straining
glacier dropped its load at the foot of the
cliff. Up that bold gray cliff the autumn
breaker bounds, roaring and splurging
with hoarse challenge, till clouds of spray
separated in the churning turmoil float up
to higher ether to make sunset nimbus,
and show the October foliage what gentle
beauty may come from harsh parentage as
well as from homes of peace.

At the foot of the cliff purling summer
coamers smooth the hard walls that resist.

The boulder, sunken but a fathom at
the flood, rises not enough to arouse the
ire of forceful antagonists, and unmoved
as sphinx to the questions of the changing
seas, it needs not to turn before the brunt,
not topple to the wooing. Now the tide

runs smoothly over it. Caught in an eddy a red seaweed whirls and spreads its shoots, and a sertularia colony swinging near has descended to mimicry of botany without putting on any air of condescension. The tremulous algæ waving from cliff to boulder and from boulder to cliff, make in the water a clear arcade, a runway. Out from a crevice glides a cautious chogset into the runway, now poising by a crimson sponge, then backing slowly underneath a translucent green sheet of sea kale. A crab makes haste to cross the round yellow bottom pebbles, carrying a burden that he fain would hide, for this is a lair, and he knows it. What is his burden, though? Oh, look, you unbelievers in disinterested friendship. 'T is a stranger crab that had to shed its armor, and unprotected needs the guarding of a friend for two whole days or more. There 's nothing "in it," as the politicians say, for the faithful protector, and yet he will not weary, but fight valiantly if necessary, and lose his very life, and for that there is no reward nor other life.

Like silver arrows a troop of spearing nervously dart from rock to wrack and from algæ to the surface, not stopping, but alert, leaving a lazy enemy no hope. What is it they fear in this quiet aisle? A slow tautog drops with the current into the runway and then as deliberately has gone.

A shrimp escaping from the sprightly pilot-fish stupidly backs straight into the clutches of a dull sea anemone at the bottom of the boulder. This is what might be called a turn in affairs. The pilot-fish knew how to catch a shrimp. The anemone did not. The anemone has the shrimp, however, and possessing now a fortune it withdraws from old friends and becomes exclusive and dis-agreeable.

A sinuous eel slides in and out among the rocks, searching for love-lorn nereid, or for mantis praying for relief from danger, which is granted till danger comes, and then he is lost, in spite of supplications, for nature cares no more for the back-sliding mantis than she does for sleek

eels.   The eel keeps near the bottom, as
though fearing.   He dreads not the blue-
fish nor bonita nor swift squeteague, for
the runway between the boulder and the
cliff is not deep enough for them.   See
them farther out, though, rising in the
curl of a mounting billow till the sun has
shot through beneath them, leaping with
an energy that goes with fish that fight
strong tides for life, not resting, never
lagging.   How dangerous such needing
maws as theirs !   An ink-laden squid
pumps faster with his siphon engine as he
steers in graceful curve through the runway.   He too suspects that it is a lurking
place.   What shadow slowly moved across
the bottom then ?   Was it from some
pausing cormorant or circling tern ?   From
this jutting storm-bleached jag of cliff I
dare to look up, but no bird flies overhead.   'T was but the shifting of the kelp
perhaps, for down in the runway waters I
see almost as clearly as through the north
wind.   'T was but the waving of sea
fronds.

Why though has all sign of life stopped

in the runway? The shadow falls across the bottom, and following it from behind the curtain of fronds there comes forth a fish so stately, so dignified in bearing, that surely he deigns not to notice these lesser fish that flee from his presence. Like a wolf he is. Not in outer likeness perhaps, but in demeanor, and in weight, and that great weight made up of all the sorts of things that swim the tide or crawl the bottom, collected by him and made to form a fish of wondrous strength, with dark straight stripes to mark the shapely sides. A clear stern eye has he, and jaw like any trap. His glistening scales are white where white, and black they are where black. Resting upon broad fins he balances beneath the sea arbor of his lair and shows no fear, but seems to be among familiar surroundings. I'll quietly toss to him a choice bit of menhaden. It slowly drifting sinks. The film of oil rises. He takes the bait and looks for more. I'll give it to him. There's a hook in it, and fastened to the hook 600 feet of hard-laid line. Down the current it settles. He spreads a broad tail and turns quizzingly sidewise to take a look, then back he bends, and turning a finely outlined nose into the tide rests again, and lets the baited hook slide by.

The sun sinking below the horizon takes one last look into the sea by a trick of angular refraction, and finding the bass all safe calmly moves away to make day elsewhere for awhile.

The chink of a migrating finch overhead, the squeak of a bat, are evening sounds, and their harmony is not marred by the splash of a hooked bass.

The moon rises. It makes a straight and lighted road through the midst of dark heaving waters. The fishes are moving on beneath the waves, the birds are flying southward overhead. I'll hoist my sail and follow the moon road between the fishes and birds and think of ways to catch the striped bass.

SUCKER DAYS.

THE shytepokes dangled their loose legs doubtingly before settling down to a wobbly perch among the red-budding tops of the soft maple saplings, but after many balancings and upstretch-ing of necks they could finally look down through the white sumacs and choose a safe alighting place in the mucky, trembling swamp where we boys never could go. It was not a large swamp; in fact, it would not strain any one very much to heave a stone half way across it now-adays, but at the time I have in mind it was a great sphagnum-lined mystery of a place, and it seemed to us youngsters that the other side was way, way over there. The boulders in the rough pastures round about it were partly hidden with chaplets of huckleberry bushes and sweet fern,

and here and there along the stone walls
some of the butternuts that a past generation of squirrels hid too well had developed into scrawny trees. Through the
leafless bushes of the swamp we could get
a glimpse of a little round pond hole out
near the middle, and tradition had it that
no one had ever found bottom there.
That was because no one had ever tried.
If any one had ever found bottom there
he surely would have told of it ; and so
the question remained as settled with us.
The swamp was just one of a thousand in
New England, but special interest cen-
tered in this one because Brown Brook
emerged from it, and with its many little
swirls and pourings and bubblings among
the bogs and rocks finally entered the old
mill-pond right where the button bushes
grew thickest.

Brown Brook was not exactly a spring
brook, because in the summer-time the
water got pretty warm, and sometimes
there wasn't very much of it anyway, and
that's why the boy of whom I am going to
write never heard from the ten small mot-

tle-backed, skittish trout that he lugged
over from Sandy Brook in a tin pail and
put into it. Possibly they are up in the
bottomless swamp hole now, and weighing
a pound or two apiece, but only the minks
know about that.

There was one thing that the brook was
good for and that was its suckers. Who
ever heard tell of a brook that was good
for nothing? In the springtime, when
the soft maples were beginning to invite
the purple finches, suckers ran up from
the mill-pond, and during the day remained beneath the large stones in the
brook. When school was out for noon
recess "us boys" had time to run over to
the brook and catch a sucker or two in
our hands by feeling for them under the
stones and then encircling them in all the
death-like grip that was possible in short,
chubby fingers. The suckers were not
very large ones, but sometimes a half-
pounder was caught, and on a day that I
want to remember all about, the boy found
an "awfully" great big one way in under a
shelving rock. Just as he was getting

ready to grab, the sucker darted out between the boy's feet and fluttered and
splashed over the ripples into another hole
farther down stream.

Any fish is to a boy something worthy
of his entire attention, and it did n't matter if the water in the hole where the big
sucker had gone was rather deep, for who
cared about getting in over the tops of
his boots when such a fish was within
reach! I don't remember exactly how
old the boy was, but probably he had not
heard the first jingling of the peep-frogs
more than eight times, and it was hard
for such small ears to notice the bell that
announced the ending of recess time, or
the calls of Ned Ellis and Joe Carroll as
they ran back to school.

The boy knew precisely under which
stone the big sucker had gone, and carefully reaching one hand beneath it he
could feel the cool, smooth sides of the
fish as it crowded a little farther in away
from him.   Then, putting the other hand
in position to head off attempts at escape,
he suddenly held the struggling, gasping

6

sucker in both hands. The stones were slippery, and in an effort to steady himself the boy partly lost his grip, and felt the sucker surely working out of his hands —you know how it feels—and despairingly tossed it toward the bank. The sucker landed among the dry pebbles, protruded his long, white nose, and opened his round mouth in surprise, and then with one ungainly flop threw himself into the brook again. Why can't a fish ever flop the other way just once? The boy in confusion could not see which way the fish went, and a moment later there was a peculiar sort of mist in the boy's eyes that prevented him from seeing much of anything, and the round drops, welling up straight from his heart, followed each other in quick succession down his cheeks.

Sorrowfully he trudged up to the schoolhouse and made wet tracks to the hard board seat in the middle of the room. That seat had seen quieter moments, when the boy had time to " fire " spit-balls upon the wall overhead, or to bore converging holes in the desk, into which various luckless flies were tucked when the teacher was looking the other way.   Miss Chapman was of the tall, austere type, and her glasses presented the only smooth outlines in her mein.   She must have been young, for her moustache was not markedly visible from the other end of the room, but her strong right arm swung with a freedom that we were accustomed to see only when the best of woodchuck skin flail strings gave security at a joint.   Usually she took off her glasses before descending to the boy's seat, but on this occasion there was too much necessity for promptness in attending to him, and they rattled upon the floor in the midst of a medley of ruler whacks and sobs.   All that afternoon and during the night visions of the big sucker filled the boy's brain to the exclusion of all other ideas, and at the woodpile at home he unconsciously made a sudden grab for the biggest stick and scattered the armful already collected.

Of course we boys all rushed off to the brook next day at recess, and while Ned and Tom and Joe went to fishing under

the stones near the road, the other boy
followed the brook down into the pasture
and began to poke under rocks in all of
the holes, to see if the big sucker was still
in that part of the stream. All at once it
rushed out in sight, and the shouts of the
boy brought the others on a run as fast as
they could come.

" Right under that stone he is, fellers,
and an old whopper, too, by golly," said
he. " I 'm going to hold on to him this
time, you bet." Just then came the sound
of the school bell across the fields. It is
called a musical sound, but somehow or
another it seems to a boy to be different
from the voices of the robins and the
wood-thrushes. Ruefully the boy paused
a moment and listened, then reaching
around and feeling the tender parts that
had not quite recovered from the previous
day's reddening, he decided that they
would have to stand one more ruling
from the bench, and into the brook he
stepped. His hands trembled with excitement as they went under the water and
under the stone and felt the fins of the

hiding sucker, but with a decision that brings results in all things he squeezed the fish in a good double grasp and carried it so far out in the meadow grass that it left all hope behind. Was n't it a beauty! We picked it up and let it flounce out of our hands a dozen times before it became submissive.

"How will you trade him for mine?" asked Tom Allen. "Oh, but that one of yours ain't anywheres near so big as this one," said the boy. "No," said Tom, "but them big ones is all innards and no meat. Just heft mine onct. There 's twicet as much meat on him." So, always ready to be taken advantage of in a bargain for any plausible reason, the boy traded the great big sucker for Tom's smaller one, and we lugged our respective fish almost to school and hid them under the stone wall. It is unnecessary to refer to our experience within the doors, but our aches were tempered with the prospective exultation of carrying the suckers home after school was out. And then an unexpected movement of the boy's mind suddenly shifted it to an impulse to give his fish to poor forlorn Uncle Bennett, whose bent back and meagre rheumatic legs tried all day long and all night long to find one soft spot in the lonely cabin down by the blacksmith shop. His wife dead, his only son a drunkard, his little hoard spent, it was with a bowed head that he accepted a bit of help from the town, and an occasional gift of a bushel of potatoes or a peck of turnips from some prosperous neighbor. He could not go to the poorhouse over the hill, where old Sperry's wife, and the blind colored cooper, and the crazy Dutchman, and Mr. Bradley's worn-out hired man, freed from the care of providing for the immediate necessities of life, had risen to a social position far superior to that of the man whose pride forced him flat against the earth. His poor old heavy heart would lift for the moment and something like light would shine through his sad blue eyes whenever we boys went in to see him, carrying from home a kind word and a batch of fallen sponge-cake

that was taken out of the oven too soon
and would not do at all for the sewing
society on Thursday evening. How much
better to give a sucker to Uncle Bennett
than to receive almost anything from
Heaven one's self. He should have the
precious fish and the family at home must
depend upon the market down in the village—as they always preferred to do.
The boy laboriously wrote on a piece of
paper torn from the soiled fly-leaf of his
speller, "lets Givum ~~two~~ too unkelbent,"
and stealthily passed the note over to
Tom Allen's desk. A quick nod of Tom's
head from behind his "joggerphy" showed
that an enterprising boy who could de-
fraud his companion because that was one
of the laws of trade, was nevertheless
unable to resist the impulse to give his
plunder to Uncle Bennett. That appeared to Tom a matter of right and
wrong in which he was governed no doubt
by the laws of compensation, because
Uncle Bennett had such a superlative degree of nothing at all.

It was almost four o'clock. Who ever

could remember the hard words in the speller right on the verge of four o'clock and freedom and good deeds! Miss Chapman slowly laid down the book that she was accustomed to hold before her face as a sort of ambush from which she surprised new scholars who thought that she was reading. The little brass desk-bell tinkled and the announcement was made that school was dismissed, excepting for the two boys who had waded in the water, and they must stay for fifteen minutes after school. One by one those fifteen rusty minutes hitched along the floor of time, and then the two impatient boys, waving their caps in the air, bounced out of the doorway and hippety-hopped over to the stone wall for their hidden treasures. Alas for the trustfulness of youth! The old gray cat had found the fish and had dragged them off to some other hiding-place.

THE EVENING OF AUG. 1, 1895.

AN Indian, a salmon, a syenite rock. The salmon lies upon the grizzly slope of syenite, and the Indian, fitting his wet moccasins to the rough foothold, rests one end of my gaff against the silvery scales of the big salmon to prevent him from sliding back into his roaring home.

The sun is setting, and for a brief moment the rays seem to warm the bleak hills of white caribou moss and the dark gullies of stunted black spruce, but the warmth is in the color only. The steel-gray clouds come westward from the ice-blocked straits of Belle Isle with a fine bracing air, but there is no suggestion of real midsummer. A white-throated sparrow among the wild peas pipes loudly to a neighbor up among the chicoutai berries and then sweetly and clearly the spiritual notes of a hermit thrush ring out farewells to the day that is passing.

The salmon has never known any other river but this one.   His mother hid the egg securely under a heap of clean sparkling sand in a shallow tributary of the river away up on the great Labrador plateau one day in October, and then hurried back to the sea before the ice caught her.   The sheldrakes and wild geese had returned in the springtime before the little salmon had worked his way out of the egg and up through the sand into the clear water of the brook.   Two years he spent in the river as a gay parr, splashing out after the ephemeridæ on the surface, scooting after the dodging stickle-backs, and slyly waiting for the small eels to venture away from their protecting stones.   Then he lost his scarlet spots, and coming down the river in smolt colors went out among the rocky islands in the Gulf of St. Lawrence, where sea plants make red and yellow thickets at the bottom. At first he caught snappy crustaceans and tender sandlaunces, and found such an abundance of food that he soon grew to proportions which enabled him to grapple with a capelin or smelt. By the end of his third year he dared to rush into a scattering school of herrings and select the fattest one for himself, and, as a trim grilse, he appeared again in the river, coming up with his older anadromous relatives on their migration. He did not have to keep an eye on the voracious sea trout now, and he escaped the seals easily because they chased the larger salmon and did not give him much attention. He felt the pride of a mature fish, however, and a superiority over his sisters, who needed to wait in the sea a longer time before they were ready to accompany him up to the old homestead in summer.

In six or seven years he became a wonderfully strong salmon, making annual trips up the river and fearing nothing but the otters and the bears when he lay in shallow currents at rest. The osprey and the golden eagle occasionally dropped

down at him from out of the sky, but they
stopped when they were near enough to
see how swift the water was in which he
rested with such apparent ease.   The on-
set of the hissing chute and the smother-
ing white water of the exploding falls were
to him nothing more than a challenge to
try his strength.   He would first leap into
the air below the falls and take a good
look at them, for they could kill him stone
dead in an instant if he were to allow it.
After looking at the falls he would run up
more closely and hold his head out of the
confusing, boiling foam for an inspection
of the easiest-looking place.   Then he
would spring six feet into the thunder,
and hurled back violently with injury to
his dignity he would gather his powers
for a mighty effort, and in one clear pa-
rabola of twelve feet or more would sail
through the air over the flying water at
the foot of the falls and force himself up
through the awful current to a resting-
place in the eddy above.

    This he would do when the day was
bright and clear, but through the night

and on dark days he would remain quietly
in favorite places where the water ran
at the rate of about two miles per hour,
over pebbles and cobble-stones. It looked
as though he remained in the open current without a motion, but on close observation one could see that his nose was
behind a cobble-stone large enough to
make a little sunken eddy, and that his
tail curved a bit from side to side.   After
mounting the first rapid near the sea he
usually spent two weeks in the pool
above, and then on ascending the second
fall he remained for a week in the next
pool, and in that way he proceeded like
any experienced traveller who has learned
how to enjoy himself and find comfort on
the road.   When he first went into the
fresh water every year his colors were
startlingly silvery, gleaming in the light
that winnowed down through the crinkles
of swift water.   Ten days later his back
and gill covers and fins began to become
blackish, and his sides were a trifle less silvery.   Two months later, at the head-
waters of the river, his colors were

distinctly black and reddish. From the first day of his entrance into the river the kipper hook on his under jaw began to grow, and his rounded sides became flatter, because he did not eat while in the river. He would often jump at a fluttering miller or a little shiner at the surface just as a kitten leaps for a ball but that would not be called eating.

Last year while passing through the estuary from the sea he was gilled in Monsieur Jules's net, but he soon thrashed himself out of that predicament, leaving a ring mark around his neck where the net had torn away the scales. Two years ago he chose the wrong spot for a leap at the falls and was thrown back over the rocks so quickly that his side was badly torn and one pectoral fin was split lengthwise. So back he went down river and into the sea until the wounds were healed, knowing that if he remained in fresh water saprolegnia would grow in the injured tissues and make him weak. He returned to the upper waters of the river in time to find a mate who did not object to his scars any more than the German maiden objects to the duel marks on the cheeks of her lover ; but it was necessary for him to drive away a ridiculous little parr and two or three rivals, one of which locked jaws with him and did not let go until he had damaged his kipper hook.

This year the scarred old veteran came up from the Gulf three weeks ago, but he waited in brackish water below the first rapid for a week until the temperature of the river had risen to 50°, and then in the first pool he did not feel much like jumping for exercise or at passing flies until the water was several degrees warmer yet. It is hard for a salmon to keep quiet for a very long time though, and one need not stand by a pool many minutes to learn if salmon are there or not.

I did not care particularly to catch this fine old fish just now because we had had sport enough for one day. First I hooked an enormous salmon that sulked at the bottom for two hours, in spite of all my efforts to move him ; and then when he was beginning to tire, the hook came away

all at once, and so easily that one won-
dered at it having held so long. Another
salmon had given me a violent chase
down the rapids and I had torn my
clothes, lost my hat, and scratched my
hands in leaping over rocks while trying to follow him ; but he finally ran out
all of 120 yards of line, whacked my rod
straight under water, and broke away.
After that I landed two large salmon and
a sea trout. No one would crave any
more physical exertion after that sort of
work, and so Jo-mul and I had gone back
to camp.

We were sitting at the edge of the rocks
in front of camp making the smelt jump at
a cast of small flies, while Caribou Charley
cooked the young murres that he had
condescended to collect for supper, along
with a pailful of cloudberries and hairy
currants. Several smelt would dart at
the flies at once, and I told Jo-mul of the
common saying among white men that
salmon fishing spoiled a man for any other
sort of sport with the rod, and asked him
if we had not many and many a time

rigged up a light rod and gone to fishing for smelt, fork-tail charrs, whitefish, sea trout, or brook trout, while a dozen leaping salmon were in sight.   Then again, after a fine salmon had been brought to gaff, we have gone down the bay and had no end of fun digging clams and pulling lobsters out from under the rocks, or we have gone up to deep water and fished on the bottom for lake trout with a plain vulgar hook and sinker, when salmon would have risen to almost any cast of the fly in the pools.   No! I am suspicious of the color of the blood of a sportsman who is ruined by salmon fishing. Nevertheless, a salmon is the greatest prize that is obtained by the fisherman.

While we sat waiting for supper an hour ago and were catching the smelts in order to fill in all chinks of time, two or three fish that looked like ouananiche began to leap and play a few yards out in the stream, so I got the salmon rod out again in order to catch one of them for identification.   The Jock Scott fly was cast gently into the smooth gliding rapid water at the head of a short but noisy chute, and when the fly rounded up and rippled the water at the end of a straightened line this great salmon unexpectedly appeared. He advanced close up to the fly, almost touched it with his blunt nose, stood poised for a moment in the current, and then turned away, making a swirl that boiled the water up in a smooth, round dome at the place where he had been an instant before. He was given time to settle back to his resting-place, and then the fly went out to search for him again. This time he came with a rush, and opening a great mouth that shut the fly in completely, he turned to disappear again; but feeling the hook and the tightening line he leaped eight feet into the air, shook his head savagely, and bending his body into a bow struck at the line with his tail while high in air. The water splashed to the shore and splattered the rocks as he splurged under again, and then with the speed of an express train he rushed fifty yards out into the river and made a graceful broad jump

of fifteen feet over the surface.   Turning
sharply down stream he shot instantly
through the chute, stopping to whirl once
in the broken water, and then pulled out
a hundred yards of line so swiftly that it
fairly took my breath away before I could
jump over the rocks and follow him along
the shore.   Up he went into the air again
and then back into the current, yanking
his head furiously back and forth with
regular strokes.   His next move was to
march up behind a rock in deep water,
where he sulked, remaining in the same
place for ten minutes, and giving nervous
twitches on the line, which was drawn so
tightly in the water that it hummed a
tune in G minor, and cut the water so
that a little transparent sheet an inch high
stood straight up.

In thirty minutes the salmon had become sufficiently tired to allow me to
guide him into shallow water near Jo-mul,
who struck him fairly with the gaff and
lifted him out upon the rock at his feet.
A beautiful fish it is, and one that required a pretty good knowledge of his

7

habits in order to take him out of the ele-
ment in which he was well equipped for
methods of escape.

As for Jo-mul, who stands there so
erect and solemn upon the rock holding
the salmon with the gaff, he too has
habits and a life history. His long black
hair is cut evenly around at the level of
his shoulders, and his straight thin nose,
high cheek-bones, and dark skin mark the
man whose ancestors were perhaps here
with the other indigenous animals. He is
not at all like a white man, although he says
that he can speak English. I asked him
if he had ever seen a moose so far north
and he replied, "Seen um be markin' on
de paper." That was an unusually good
and long answer for him. As a rule it is
necessary to ask him a question several
times before he makes any kind of an
answer in Montagnais, traders' French,
or English. He is not morose, but like
others of his race he has failed to develop
the bump of language. I do not remember to have seen him laugh but once, and
that was when I asked him to cut enough

firewood to last for several days. It was a good joke. Nothing appeals to an Indian's sense of the ludicrous like the idea of laying up anything in advance. He tries to imitate Caribou Charley and me in some things, and I do not dare to leave my tooth-brush out or he surely would try it. He still prefers to lean over the river Narcissus-like when parting his hair in the morning instead of using our more civilized mirror, which is made by sinking a rubber coat-tail in a pan of water.

Every year in July Jo-mul comes down to the coast and disposes of his canoe load of furs to some trader. A fine black mink skin is worth two dollars, so for that the trader gives him a five-cent pipe on which he has placed the value of two dollars. His skins of beaver, otter, fox, marten, lynx, fisher, wolverine, and bear are traded off for pickles, Florida water, gunpowder, tobacco, and the simplest necessaries in the way of clothing and provisions, but usually to pay the last year's debt ; and the things that he wants are advanced to him, for he is known as an honest Indian.

That means that he has learned that advances will not be made unless debts are paid. An Indian is apt to be relatively honest. Jo-mul would probably not steal a gold watch because he does not know what it is good for, but it would not be safe to leave a pound of pork near him. He would cross himself with one hand while purloining the pork with the other, for the missions have not been without their influence in this region.

Jo-mul has a wife and two children, but his ideas of family are not troublesome, and he would not feel so very badly if some young brave were to run off with his comely daughter before marriage, especially if the young brave could furnish food enough and would give the daughter a bright red ribbon or two. After Jo-mul has traded off his furs and has lain about camp for four or five weeks the family start off on their annual trip into the interior, to come down the river in the following year just as the salmon are going up. Jo-mul has few motives or ambitions beyond those of any of the other large animals of this latitude. He would never think of making a pet of any wild animal. He would not live a moral life for its own reward, because there would be some difficulty in explaining to him the nature of that reward. He would not be content with four meals a day if he could get eight, and he does not feel like working when he is full of food and wants to sleep.

He seems to live for the purpose of completing a round of life. One round begins with the water bacteria which are eaten by infusoria, which are eaten by mollusks, which are eaten by fish, which are eaten by Jo-mul, who will be eaten by bacteria in turn if he is not careful in shooting the rapids. Another round begins with the land plants, which are eaten by the caribou, which are eaten by Jo-mul, who will be eaten by the bacteria and turned over to the land plants again if he is careful about shooting the rapids. Thus will Jo-mul fill his place in the economy of nature, and apparently there is no other mission for him on earth,

The syenite rock is about the only thing near camp which has no habits. It lies there partly submerged beneath the sullen current. It is waiting.

.

IN THE SANDY END OF
A CONNECTICUT
TOWNSHIP.

"THAT nigh mare is a cribber, is n't she, Jim?

"Cribber? Why goddlemitey, yes. All the hosses up this way is cribbers; or most on 'em is, cause the air is so gol darned good up here that they want to suck 'emselves full of it and keep sucked full, besides what they kin git into their innards reg'lar ways. Say! you 'd better come up here to stay fer a spell and you 'd git as healthy as a hoss. Whoa thar, Jinny! Whoa thar, Lije! Git on here quick, you fellers. Whoa, Lijah! Aint this a mornin' fer trout, though? Sling them baskets and poles in and git fixed as soon 's you kin."

" Little bit frisky this morning, are n't they, Jim ? "

"Stiddy thar, Jinny ! Oh, that 's nothin'. I 'll run 'em up Bald Hill lickety split and they 'll stand while we 're fishin' after that. Say ! Look here ! Don't let yer feet swing too fur from the front of the waggin so 's to hit Jinny's legs."

" Is she a kicker, Jim ? "

" Kicker ? Well, no ; not zactly, 'less you begin it yerself. Be a little keerful, though. Oh, never mind 'bout movin' back. Stay whar you be. Don't get skeered. She won't kick 'less she 's s'prised. I 've only jist got her, and I 'll treat her kinder kind, and bimeby she won't never kick. Git up, Jinny ! "

Jim accompanied the injunction with a cobble-stone which he pulled out of his side pocket, striking the mare between the ears.

" Git up ! "

Another stone from the side pocket hit her on the neck.

" Why do you do that, Jim ? Why don't you use your whip ? "

" Whip! Can't use no whip on her.
I jist carry along a pocket full of stuns
and tetch her up ahead a leetle.   That 's
whar she needs it.   Don't need no stir-
rin' up behind.   Too gol darned smart
there aready."

" Where did you buy her, Jim ?"

" Buy her ?   I haint never bought no
·hosses. Aint no use a-buyin' 'em. Traded.
Allers traded ! Leastways, most allers
traded.   They 's men that 'll pay a hundred dollars cash down fer a hoss, but
them folks can't get ahead none. Bought
my fust hoss, come to think.   I was down
to Stony Creek and they was a-loadin' a
schooner fer York, and the feelin' come
over me all to once that I wanted to go
fur a travel, and I says to the cap'n, says I :

" ' Cap'n, what 'll you take to let me go
to York with you ?'

" ' Come on, Jim,' says he, 'and help
me load up and I 'll take you down and
back if you 'll help both ways.'

" That 's how I got my start.   Kinder
curis, aint it, how a feller 'll git a start from
a feelin' that comes over him and he 's in a

handy spot fur the feelin'. Well, we got down to York, and one day while he was a-waitin' I come to a hoss-car track in the road, and bein' kinder curis, I follered it up and bimeby I come to a big stable and the gol dumbedest pile of horses that ever you seen. Bimeby they onhitched a hoss that come in kinder lame and dumpish, and the hoss doctor he looked him over and he says to the boss, says he :

"'Sudden attack of spilin'-men-an-cheat-us. Hoss busted,' says he.

" Then they went away, and I histed up that hoss's off hind leg and I seen that ere spilin'-cheat-us lodged in under the shoe, and it wa'n't no bigger 'n a robin's egg. I did n't pry it out just then, but I kinder waited round, and bimeby I went up to the boss and I says :

"'What 'll you take fer that hoss ?'

"' Take fifty,' says he, thinkin' he was cheatin' me.

" Them city fellers 'll cheat you quicker 'n a wink. Nothin' agin you fellers, 'cause you aint thar now.

"' Give you five,' says I.

" ' Twenty-five,' says he.

" ' Six,' says I.

" ' Give me eight and take him,' says he.

" So I give him eight and had three dollars left in my pocket.   Made it burnin' charcoal summer before, and was lookin' fer a chance to speckerlate, never thinkin' 't would come unexpected like that. Well, when I got down the road I pried out that 'ere cheat-us and got the hoss aboard the schooner and got him up here, and from that start I 've been tradin' and tradin' and I 've had lots of hosses and waggins and harnesses, besides a purty good livin'.'

" Ever get any bad horses, Jim ? "

" Bad uns?   Why, no, not r-e-e-l bad."

" How did the dashboard get knocked out of the buggy up at the house ? "

" Kicked out, I s'pose ! "

" Bad horse ? "

" No ; not r-e-e-l bad !   Can't remember jest which one it was. Long time ago."

" What did you feed the horse, on board the schooner ? "

" Hay ! "

" Where did you get hay ? "

" Oh, they was a lot of it on the dock all done ·up fancy.   Good hay though. Smelt of it."

" Whose hay was it ? "

" Dunno ! "

" I wish we could fish the old Howell brook this morning, Jim ; but they say that a club has bought rights and posted it.   How do you like that sort of thing here in this part of the country ? "

" Like it ?   Why, fust rate.   Ketched bigger trout and more of 'em than ever before."

" But don't you ever run across the watchman ? "

" Oh, lordy, yes !   Run acrost him more 'n forty times."

" But did n't he stop you ? "

" Stop me ? "—and Jim's voice sounded like the sudden breaking of a bed slat— " Stop me ?   Why, no.   He knows I kin lick him quicker 'n lightnin'.   Allers licked him at school when we was boys.   But I 've got a brook all posted for you fellers.   Three miles on it."

"I did n't know that you owned so much land, Jim."

"I don't own none o' that land," said Jim; "but you see it 's this way. Them club fellers got a notion of comin' over to this brook, so I went and stuck up a lot of signs."

"But how about the owners?"

"Well, you see how it is; the land up here 's mortgaged 'way up, and the men what 's on the farms thinks that the mortgagers put up them signs, and the mortgagers thinks that the men what 's on the farms put 'em up, and bein' a leetle skeered of each other, they don't ask no questions."

"So you did not have to pay anything?"

"No; nothin'. They aint no money up this way to pay for things nohow, so we hev to do the best we kin without money. Money aint nec'ssary fer folks with heads on 'em. It 's fer dudes. Nothin' agin you fellers — cause — cause — praps you haint got much on it. They was a feller up here had two hundred and forty-six dollars saved up, burnin' charcoal, and he was awful skeered that some un would ketch him and git it—wuss 'n a mink with a black hide—and so he slept over in that charcoal hut over yender—'way from folks.'"

" Did they find him, Jim ? "

" Yep ! "

" Get his money ? "

" Yep !   Killed him."

" Was it known who did it ? "

" Yep !   Seen the feller what done it down to the railroad station t'other day."

" But did n't they arrest him ? "

"Oh, yep !   Took him over to Hartford and tried him fer it.   Could n't prove nothin', cause he was jest that fool fer luck, that they wa' n't nobody lookin' on when he done it, so he was 'quitted. When I seen him t'other day down to the station, I walked up to him and I says, says I :

" ' Gabe, you know gol·darned well that you was the feller that killed Mart.' "

" What did he say to that, Jim ? "

"Oh, he says, ' Git out,' says he, and poked me in the ribs with his thumb.   He knows me fust rate, you know. Wish you fellers 'd go up to Hall's pond some day and ketch some of them black bass that was put in up there."

"Have you tried them, Jim?"

"Yep! Tried 'em with that purty little trout pole you give me three years ago."

"Catch any?"

"Dunno!"

"A man usually knows whether he has caught a bass or not."

"Well, it's this way. You see I put on a frog and hove him out by a good-lookin' rock, and all to oncet they was a yell of a yank, and I pulled my all firedest, and the bass he pulled his all firedest, and bimeby somethin busted, and I haint got that purty leetle pole now. Next time I go bassin' I'll take along a bean pole, and a purty gol darned stubbed one at that."

"We will write to you if we find that we can come up again this spring for the bass, Jim."

"'T won't do no good to write."

"Why not?"

"Cause old Hank, the postmaster, he's

got a grudge agin me. Last year he sent
word over they was a letter fer me to the
post-office, and said he would n't give it to
me till I licked him fer it. He would n't
let me have it fer two weeks just to tan-
terlize me, but I found out what was in it,
cause his woman she opened it and told
some of my folks, so he wa'n't so gol
darned smart as he thought he was."

    *   *   *   *   *   *

"Guess I 'll hitch up Syb to take you
fellers down to the station this mornin'.
Sorry you can't stay and git another big
mess like yest'day. Like to hev you
round. Thar 's Mary, she goes and slicks
up when you 're round jest like when I
was courtin' her. They 's lots of trout
too. Why, I ketched one over by Barnes's
t' other day that weighed a pound and a
half. Pound an' a half, wa'n't it, Mary?"

"Two pound, plumb, James."

"And then up there to the hog hole I
ketched, l'e's see, 't was some thirty-odd,
wa'n't it, Mary?"

"Forty-eight, James." (Loyalty, thy
name is woman!)

"Get in, boys.   Springs a leetle weak
for three, but Syb don't mind if anything
busts."

"That's a pretty mare, Jim, where did
you get her?"

"Traded!   Traded with a feller over
to Madison when she was a colt.   Aint
she a beaut?"

"What does the name Syb stand for,
Jim?"

"Sybil!"

"How in the name of goodness did you
ever come to name a colt Sybil?"

"Sybil?   Why, that was the name of
the gal of the feller I got the colt of.
Sech a gol darned purty gal, I named
the colt after her, knowin' it must grow
up beautiful with sech a name."

"Do you know what a sibyl is, Jim?"

"No.   It must be somethin' too gol
darned sweet and beautiful fer these parts,
'ceptin' as I 've got it in that mare."

Sybil was really a most beautiful and
intelligent little mare, and Jim had made
her his pet.   The tenderness that his
knotty hands displayed in managing her

8

and the soft voice in which he spoke to
her were very touching, and she, like a
spoiled girl, did just as she pleased, but
with the evident intention of reciprocating
Jim's affection.   She wore no blinders and
went along the sandy road at any gait
that happened to please her for the moment.   The little mare would leisurely jog
off to one side of the road to keep in the
shade of the maples, and then deliberately
cross over to trot in the shade of the but-
ter-nuts on the other side, if that was the
better side.   She threw her head around
over her shoulder and looked straight at
Jim when he spoke to her, meanwhile not
changing her gait.   She stopped a moment
to rub noses with a cow near the road and
then went on again without command.
Passing an old stone wall, Syb stopped so
quickly that we were almost pitched out,
and with ears pricked up she reached her
head over the fence to look at something.

"What is it, Jim?" I asked.

"Woodchuck rustlin' in the leaves, I
guess. [Standing up to look.] Yep!
woodchuck! G' long, Syb!"

"What will you take for that mare, Jim!"

"Take fer her?   No, sir-e-e.   She aint to sell.   That 's talkin' 'bout the soul, or leastways as near as I ever git to it. G' long, darlin'!"

A DAY WITH THE GROUSE.

ON one of those clean, northerly, transparent November mornings, when the elfin frost sketchers had left the tops of the kitchen window-panes sufficiently clear to give an impressionist effect of yellow sassafras leaves in the yard and embers of autumn over beyond upon the mountain side, John and I moved our creaky old-fashioned chairs up to the farm-house table and fortified ourselves for the prospective hunt with hot buckwheat cakes and sausage gravy, with home-made sausages that had spluttered and burst in the frying-pan and then turned all crunchy where their contents had quickly browned, and finally, with a warmer of coffee containing blobs of real cream and doubtful sugar.

We were clad in stout canvas hunting

suits, flannel shirts, thick hob-nailed bro-
gans, and corduroy caps ; and if any one
doubted our intentions for the day they
should have seen Don and Belle, the two
setters, as they rapped the table legs with
their tails, and poking their heads into
our laps with impatient whines looked up
with that intense expression that one sees
when the dog realizes that his master is
all ready for a hunt. Honest old Foghorn, the hound, sat in droop-eared dignity with bowed head near the stove,
looking at us occasionally out of the
corners of his eyes and hoping that he
would be invited to follow, but knowing
full well that when we were out after
grouse it was his day to remain at home.
One who has not lived and loved with
well-bred dogs cannot appreciate their
keen perceptions and their quick divina-
tion of many of the master's thoughts and
intentions. The ordinary observer would
have said that Foghorn did not care to
go with us on that day, and that the other
dogs were wistful because such was their
habit, but not a word had been spoken

to them and they all judged of our plans for the day from something in our manner that the gift had not been given us to realize ourselves. Dogs seem to see their masters' thoughts, and their deductions are all made while the philosopher is waiting for something more definite; and although the quickness of their conclusions is antagonistic to good analyses of our motives, they turn at each limitation of their understanding to a friendly supposition, and it is with a wag of the tail instead of a growl that they await further information. I respectfully refer philosophers to the dogs.

We were not out of the door before Don and Belle had bounced through ahead of us, and the frightened hens about the stone steps ran and flew ca-dark-ut-ing in great confusion back to the barnyard and over the fence into the orchard. A chilly crow unhunched himself from a frosty rail and flopped heavily along over the fields of corn-shocks and ungathered pumpkins, and out of the stiff frozen grass fluttered a few migrating sparrows as we rustled noisily along through the windrows of dead leaves in the path.   High up on the hill-tops the sun was just beginning to mingle with the few brilliant leaves that still clung to the maples, and down in the valley a line of haze above the dark pines marked the course of the stream that had been so interesting to us in the trout season.   It was a rough climb through the woods to the upper grounds where we intended to hunt, and the air was provocative of such energetic movements that we were in a glow when the high levels and the morning sunshine were reached.   Away to the right of us stretched a series of beech and chestnut ridges, with many acres of thick pines and hemlocks, while the edges of the woodland were lined with brush-lots of young poplars, birches, sumacs, and witch hazel ; patches of reddish buckwheat stubble here and there adjoined the saplings.   To the hunter's eye buckwheat stubble is the finishing touch of beauty in a landscape.

Festoons of grape-vines hung from the hornbeams in the gullies, and the ground in many places was thickly carpeted with wintergreens and princess pine. In the débris of the very first crumbling log we found a group of four wallow holes and a loose grouse-feather that looked as though it had been recently shaken out. Neither Don nor Belle made any signs of game just there, but they ranged eagerly back and forth to the loose heaps of brush, through clumps of sapling pines and along the stump fence, until the rapid wagging of Don's tail as he hesitated for a moment in the cart-path showed that a grouse had been along there that morning. For several minutes Don was busy in trying to determine the direction of the trail, but gradually becoming convinced he started off cautiously through the scrubby oak bushes with elevated nose and swinging tail. We could see his nostrils dilate and hear him snuffing, as with half-closed eyes his every energy seemed concentrated in the delicate effort of catching the floating scent. How lightly he stepped as he led us off toward a fallen tree-top! And then he began to grow stiff-legged, and stopped.

His tail straight out : every muscle rigid : and his right foot lifted from the ground. Belle, seeing that he had found a bird, bounded up so hurriedly that the grouse rushed out and disappeared behind a pine before we could shoot. Out from under a scrub-oak went another grouse, and neither of the guns happened to be ready,

It was necessary to call Belle in and scold her for being so careless, and her drooping ears and tail showed that her feelings were hurt more than they would have been if we had punished her. The direction that one of the birds had taken led us out to a sumac thicket on a knoll. Both dogs were making signs of game and trying to locate the birds, when suddenly out of the ferns at my very feet burst a great gray cock grouse and sprang whir-ring into the air, shaking the saplings with his wings and whisking a circle of loose dead leaves into the air of his wake. The instant that the gun-stock struck my shoulder and the trigger was simultane-ously and intuitively pulled, the feath-ers flew in a puff, the powerful bird dropped headlong through a thorn-bush, and struck the ground with a thump, leaving a few loose feathers hanging lightly among the twigs, while dried thorn-leaves rattled down from limb to limb as they followed the bird. The empty shell in the gun was quickly replaced by a loaded one and Don was given the order to fetch. How proudly he came trotting toward us, tossing the prize upward in order to get a better hold as he ran, and at the same time being careful not to muss the feathers. His eyes were not for a moment taken from the limp grouse in my hand until its tail had disappeared in the capacious hunting-coat pocket.

Along the edge of a buckwheat stubble both dogs worked ambitiously back and forth, following first one trail and then another until we were convinced that a whole covey of grouse had been gleaning there and that their tracks were so inter-mingled that the dogs had a difficult riddle to solve. We were making a wide detour of the field when it was noticed all at once that Belle was standing on a "dead point"

at a small wisp of foxtail grass and ragweeds, and Don was a few yards away backing her.   The idea that a whole big grouse
could hide in such cover without being
visible seemed ridiculous, but we had entire confidence in the two mute authorities
standing there so motionless in the stubble, and as I walked up to Don a grouse
sprang like a new revelation out of the
wisp and started off with plenty of room
to gain all needful headway.   The first
charge of shot loosened a couple of wing
feathers and the second shot sent the bird
bounding all in a bunch among the seedy
ragweeds.   Just then two more clucking
and squealing grouse with spread tails and
half-opened wings unexpectedly appeared
and ran straight toward me, mounting on
wing so close that I could almost have
touched them with the gun.   Another one
jumped from the wisp straight up high
into the air, and a moment later two red
fellows whirred away side by side low over
the field.   A volcano and earthquake of
grouse!   There I stood with unloaded
gun and trying so hurriedly to get two

cartridges into the breech that they would not have gone into a peck measure just then. If my efforts at being wise had ever been so severe and so energetic as my efforts to get those cartridges into the breech in time for a shot, the nineteenth century would have had its Solomon.

One of the birds scudding down the wind past John suddenly folded itself up in mid air, and a long shot at another so surprised the bird that it wheeled and alighted in a hemlock at the edge of the field.

In brush lot and in bark slashing and from hill-top to swale we found grouse that day, and when in the long shadows of the thin sunlight on a cold-waxing autumn evening we reached the farm-house and spread our birds out upon the woodshed floor, the dogs, with ears full of burrs and memories replete with good deeds, curled up contentedly behind the stove for the night.

The cider in the blue pitcher that was set upon the table after supper helped to strengthen many of the weak points in the yarns of the old settler who had dropped in to tell us of the three coons that he had found in one tree that day, and Grandad Bradtree, leaning his sunken cheek on the trembling hand that balanced the cane against the arm-chair, was encouraged to tell again such stories of his exploits in the good old days as are usually reserved for grandchildren and withheld from contemporaries.

I know the beds of Eastern princes, and the luxurious couches of Occidental plutocrats, but under the rafters of a farm-house in western New York, where the mud wasp's nest answers for a Rembrandt and the cobweb takes the place of a Murillo, there is a feather bed into which the hunter who has killed a dozen ruffed grouse in the day softly sinks until his every inch is soothed and fitted, and settling down and farther down into sweet unconsciousness, while the screech owl is calling from the moonlit oak and frost is falling upon the asters, stocks may fluctuate and panic seize the town, but there is one man who is in peace.

NEPIGON AND SAGUENAY RIVERS.

A FIVE-MINUTES' COMPARISON.

THE Nepigon River has for its source a great spring which presses against more than ninety miles of encircling rocks in seeking for a chance to escape, and then pours heaps of canorous water pell-mell through a forty-mile chute straight into diaphanic Lake Superior. If the river stops a bit wherever there is need to touch up the landscape with a lake, or if it runs slowly past engaging scenery, no one cares very much, because it makes up for lost time in a headlong chase over the rocks all of the rest of the way.

The Saguenay River, with its forty miles of tannate water debouching into a dark sullen estuary, is the result of a conference of long rivers which meet at Lake St.

John and require ninety miles of sandy
circumference for the assembly.   If you
would know which St. John the lake is
named after, try to cross it in a birch-bark
canoe when a question of north wind is
before the conference.   The Nepigon
River, as a strong individual character,
retains its original motives and carries
into Lake Superior the same volume of
clearest cold water with which it started,
—water that makes such white foam and
spray in the rapids that the Indians could
not help calling the river the Nepi-gon, or
river-that-is-like-snow.   Such a river is not
very susceptible to passing influences, and
during the whole year it may not rise or
fall more than twenty-five inches, while the
Saguenay, responding to many influential
constituents, rises and falls as many feet
in the course of two months, and not only
that, but it is warm or cold at the dictation
of the season.

The Nepigon is not afraid to show its
true nature at the outset of its career,
and it gives honest warning that it is powerful.   The Saguenay, on the other hand,

leaves the St. John Conference with mur-
der in its heart. Stealthily as a leopard
it noiselessly glides to the Isle d'Alma,
then it mutters and growls for a while, and
suddenly bursts out with demoniacal fe-
rocity upon the rocks in its path.   If you
are a master of rivers and fear none of
them, go to the Nepigon and to the
Saguenay and see how grandly nature is
displayed along these two great tributa-
ries of the St. Lawrence which are so
much alike upon the map and so different
in their characters.   Leave behind the
pleasures of the city that are dependent
upon arts which stimulate the mind
without nourishing the soul; where the
gardener makes the rose more and more
beautiful as he gradually forces its stamens
to become petals, until, as the queen of
flowers, it has lost the power of generation; where the arts of civilization
stimulate the mind until it flames up in
genius and a degenerate body falls back.
Go to the Nepigon and to the Saguenay
and see what substantial things can be
found there in nature.   On the Nepigon,

igneous cliffs of trap rock tower in stern
grandeur over the river-that-is-like-snow.
The dark forest growth of fir and tama-
rack, toned by poplar, birch, and round-
wood, becomes thinned and sparse on the
mountains, just as though the Oreads had
planned their forest before violent up-
heavals of the earth made ten humpy miles
out of one smooth mile, and thereby upset
their calculations. On the Saguenay—the
corrupted name for the Shagahneu-hi, or
ice-hole river, so named because the seals
used to keep many air-holes open in the
ice of the estuary—Laurentian rocks in
sombre piles lift up their covering of
coniferous and deciduous trees, which are
much like those of the Nepigon, but here
and there a fine yellow pine holds mo-
narchial possession of a jagged island, and
the trunks of the northern white birch
light up the forest aisles. An area of fos-
siliferous limestone on Lake St. John has
come to the surface, bearing evidence of
the abundance of life in Silurian days. A
devout clergyman remarked that these
fossils were never alive, but were placed

there in their present form to test our
faith, and they have done it.   Moose and
caribou sometimes leave tracks among
the twin-flowers and adder-mouths along
the banks of both the Nepigon and Saguenay rivers, and one need not go very far
away to find abundance of such game.
Black bears swim the rivers at safe cross-
ing-places, and the voice of a gray wolf
may be heard above the sound of rushing
waters when all else under the stars is
still.   Along both rivers the northern
hares furnish the principal food supply
for carnivorous animals and birds, just as
the ciscoes furnish a large food supply for
the predatory fishes of the region. Spruce
grouse and ruffed grouse fly into the bushes
near the fisherman, and look at him in
wonderment, and the cinereous owl catches
ptarmigans on the hills in winter.   In the
Nepigon River brook trout find such an
abundance of food and such agreeably
cold water that they grow to an enormous
size, and are ready to spring after the fly at
almost any time of day after 10 o'clock in
the morning. Like fish in other very cold

streams, they do not rise readily in the
early morning, and the best sport may be
had with them in the middle of the sun-
shiniest day.   The big 6-pounders jump
at the fly almost as eagerly as the youngsters do, and the very largest trout are so
sleek and fat that they are delicious for
the camp table—quite different from the
mill-pond trout of warmer waters, which
lose flavor and activity as soon as they
have passed the ounces period in their
lives.   Side by side with the trout are
swarms of monstrous pike (*Esox lucius*),
and sometimes one of these will take a
silver-doctor fly.   So will the salmon trout
which lurk in the tail water of deep rapids, and so will the pike-perch if one is
casting the fly at night.   The Nepigon
looks like good bass water from the fisherman's point of view, but the bass themselves say that it is too cold, and I know
of only two that have been caught there.

If we leave the best trout water to itself
for a while and toss the fly over still black
reaches where the water is ever so many
fathoms deep, a surprise may come to the

surface in the form of a pale trout with translucent nose and fins, who shows by his colors that he lives away down in the gloom of bottom caverns. We must not expect to catch one of these trout, but once in a while there comes an hour when they are all at the surface.

Whitefish take the fly readily if one is knowing enough to tempt them in a politic way, and they certainly belong to the game fishes of America. They cannot chase and capture an ordinary artificial fly, but if we put half a dozen flies, tied on No. 14 hooks on a single leader, and drop this affair lightly among the fins that are circling about at the surface in the evening, and keep it perfectly still, pretty soon the whitefish will move up to it and try to pick off the small flies as daintily as a red deer nips a lily bud.

Although there are half a dozen species of fish that will rise to the fly in the Nepigon, the chief game fish of the river is first and last the red-spotted square-tailed brook trout. In the Saguenay the chief game fish is the ouananiche, or so-called landlocked salmon. This is the inland salmon that is found in many lake streams from Maine to Labrador, if the streams contain smelts. Ichthyologists find the landlocked salmon anatomically much like the salmon that goes to the sea, but the ouananiche are content to remain with the food supply that is in sight in fresh water; just as certain people who might be important in the city prefer to remain small in the village, because they are satisfied with the opportunities in sight, though anatomically they are the same folks. It is principally a question of size of opportunity.

In the Saguenay we find the same monstrous pike and the same pike-perch and whitefish as in the Nepigon, but the trout are absent. There are plenty of trout in the tributary streams which are not inhabited by the ouananiche, but the two fish rather avoid each other because they are such close rivals. Both are magnificent, but they cannot see it in each other.

The guides of the Nepigon are for the

most part Chippewa Indians or half-breeds, who are willing enough to have visitors enter their domain, but who are not very amiable. Such is their nature. They do not even make friends of their dogs, who would gladly love them and forgive all of their failings. A stray Indian dog of the most pathetic yellow color came to our camp one day, and when we tried to pat his head the poor little fellow spread his legs apart and braced himself, thinking that we were trying to push him over. He did not know that there was any such thing as affection in the whole round world ; but we developed that latent trait for him, and glad indeed was he to find at the end of a week that his tail had a use and that it could wag.

On the Saguenay the guides are hardy, polite French-Canadians, simple in their ways, and delighted to have a chance to show their hospitality if we visit their humble homes. In their relations with each other every man stands on his real merits and accepts the position that is given him in the estimation of his *con-*

frères. Monsieur E. R. Dutou cannot block
up a shaky reputation by signing himself
Eelnavo Reanne Dutou. He cannot ele-
vate the neighborhood by forcing his name
under society in the form of a wedge as
E. Reanne Dutou ; nor can he send the
chain-shot name of Eelnavo Reanne-
Dutou hurtling through a startled public
if he is personally deficient in powder.

The Nepigon has completed its duty
when the tribute of waters is freely paid
to Lake Superior, but the Saguenay
avariciously makes its current pass
through a long estuary before deliver-
ing its property to the sea. The estuary is full of weird interest. The
sombre current, the beetling mountains,
and the cold northern air are all in keeping. White whales gleam out of the dark
flood in striking contrasts of color. A
beluga is not "sort of white," but is one
of the most beautiful of white animals, the
quality of his coloring reminding one of
the soft, supple white of a pure white
stallion.

At Tadousac, with its lofty terraces of

shifting dunes, the Saguenay joins the St. Lawrence grudgingly, and the reddish waters push far out into those of the greater river before their moroseness is tamed.

A Note on Tannate Water.

Wishing to have an explanation for the reddish stain of many northern streams, I wrote for information to the Department of Agriculture at Washington and at Ottawa. From Washington came the reply that no information on that subject was obtainable. From Ottawa I received a personal letter from Secretary H. B. Small, who kindly stated that while no definite answer could be given, it was his impression that the stain was due to the action of tannin in the water, and that the question would be referred to the chemists and botanists of the Department of Agriculture of Canada. A report from Chief Chemist F. T. Schutt contained analyses of Ottawa River water showing that the coloring of that river was largely due to

peaty matter held in suspension, but there
is no peat on some of the reddest streams
that I have fished, so acting upon the suggestion of Secretary Small I made experi-
mental test-tube tannates of iron and of
manganese in weak aqueous solution. The
iron tannate was at first redder than stream
water and the manganese tannate was too
smoky. A combination of equal parts of
solution of iron tannate and of manganese
tannate gave at first too smoky a color,
but after standing exposed to the light
for a few hours an abundant flocculent
precipitate formed in all of the test tubes,
and all of the solutions assumed a tint
quite characteristic of that of the streams.
This stain was little changed at the end of
two weeks. Rain water coming in contact with dead tannin-bearing trees and
plants would take tannin into solution,
and this solution percolating through a
soil containing iron or manganese would
make highly colored tannates of the met-
als before reaching a stream. Even in
peaty waters the color could be due in
part to the presence of tannates. It was

a pleasure to feel that my nice red streams were not unclean, and that they apparently represented nothing more than a pretty reaction in Nature's laboratory. It is true enough that nothing in science is unclean, but a trout is particular and would a-little rather know that the tinting of his water came from neat tannates of iron and manganese.

THE NUMBER NINE AS A TALE VARNISHER.

THE number nine is apparently the numeral of hyperbole. It is used in the place of a lesser numeral in a careless way to fill gaps in the memory of the story-teller, and it is also employed intentionally for impressive effect.

Curiously enough the use of the number nine for purposes of exaggeration has been employed since early days in history. One's attention having been attracted to the subject, it is a source of surprise to observe to what frequent use the chosen numeral is put.

A boatman who takes me out on hunting and fishing excursions is in the habit of using the number nine so often in speaking of the numbers or weight of fish and game that the listener soon perceives that he is allowing the numeral in question to stand for a lesser number of birds, or pounds of fish. In my boatman's inaccurate memory the number nine rounds out the bag to a satisfactory extent.

Beyond my amusement at this man's fibs, the subject caused no reflection until one day when off for a walk I met a man who had not succeeded in killing any snipe on that day but who said that he had killed nine on the previous evening. A little farther on a man who was fishing for bass said that he had caught only nine. On asking him to let me see them he said that they were in a scap net in the spring where they would keep cool, and on lifting out the net I found seven bass. The fisherman then decided that his wife must have come down and taken two of them to the house for dinner without his knowing it. Before reaching home that day I found a man who had killed nine ducks before breakfast just across the way from the boat-house. It then occurred to me that I was on the verge of an observation, and there came to mind at once a number of familiar nines that have been handed down to us.   A stitch in time saves nine. Nine tailors make a man.   A nine-days' wonder.   A cat has nine lives.   A cat o'nine tails.   The nine days' fast.   The nine-days' prayer.   Ninebark is the name of a plant, *Spiræa opulifolia*, in which the bark separates into several layers.   Nine killer is the name of a shrike, *Collurio borcalis*, which suspends several small objects of prey upon thorns and twigs. Nine-day fits is the name for a disease, *Trismus nascentium*.   Nine was the number of books that the Sibyl laid before Tarquin.   The Muses were nine.

We can almost formulate a law that when an exaggerator deals with numerals ranging up to eight he instinctively finds that the number nine represents the imaginative value of such numerals.   One can often take up a copy of a daily newspaper and find that reporters are fond of the number nine.   The following clippings are to the point.   While the number nine is used by various classes of people hyperbolically, it is most often heard when sportsmen are relating their tales, and it occurs so persistently in the sportsmen's papers that I instinctively glance over game and fish reports before reading them for the purpose of picking out the nines.   Three and seven are favorite numbers, but are not used like nine for hyperbole.

"NINE KNOWN TO BE KILLED.

"FIFTEEN OTHER MINERS BURIED IN THE YORK FARM COLLIERY NEAR POTTSVILLE.

"ANOTHER TERRIBLE MINE EXPLOSION IN THE READING COAL FIELD.

"The Cause of the Disaster Unknown, but it is Supposed that the Miners Struck a 'Feeder' and Ignited the Gas with their Lamps—Women and Children at the Mine's Mouth —The Work of Rescue Pushed Rapidly.

"[SPECIAL TO THE 'WORLD.']

"POTTSVILLE, PA., July 23.—York Farm Colliery, situated about two miles from this city, was the scene of a terrible explosion about noon to-day. Eight men are known to have been killed outright, and it is believed that fifteen more have suffered the same fate.   Those known to have been killed are as follows :

"1. John Harrison, of Wadesville (fire boss) ; leaves a widow and four children.

"2. Thomas Jones, Minersville ; married.

"3. William Jones, Minersville ; single.

"4. William Wehman, Minersville.

"5. James Hartzel, Llewellyn.

"6. George Kreiss, Middle Creek.

"7. Herman Werner, St. Clair ; leaves a widow and eight children.

"8. Anthony Putchlavage, Pottsville.

"Those known to have been injured are :

"Anthony Stock, boy, leg broken and burned ; . . . "

"NINE PERSONS WERE KILLED, AND THE INJURED LIST IS A LONG ONE.

"A Dense Fog Prevailed at the Time, and the Accused Engineer Claims he could not See the Signals—Rear Coach of the Passenger Train Smashed, and Few of the Travellers Escaped Uninjured—List of the Dead.

"[SPECIAL TO THE 'WORLD.']

"BOSTON, MASS., Sept. 13.—To a dense fog and apparent carelessness on the part of the engineer of the freight train is to be charged the fatal accident on the Fitchburg Railroad shortly before 11 o'clock last evening, at West Cambridge, by which eight were killed and many injured.

"The dead are :

"1. Adams, Miss Margaret, 35 years, Watertown.

"2. Barnes, John H., 61 years, Newtown.

"3. Feyler, Miss Rhita, 23 years, Waltham.

"4. Hudson, John, 51 years, Watertown.

"5. Lane, John, 46 years, Watertown.

"6. Merrifield, H. F., Watertown.

"7. Raymond, Leon O., freight brakeman, Winchendon.

"8. Sullivan, Standish P., 56 years, East Watertown.

"Following is a complete list of the injured. . . ."

"NINE HAT FACTORIES REOPENED.

"BUT IT IS SAID THAT FEW OF THE OLD EMPLOYÉS HAVE RETURNED TO WORK.

"[BY TELEGRAPH TO THE 'HERALD.']

"DANBURY, CONN., Jan. 25, 1894.—Nine of the twenty hat factories that have been closed two months by a lockout of their employés reopened this morning. The manufacturers refuse to tell how many of their late employés returned, but the Executive Committee of the unions places the total number at twenty-two. The firms that reopened their factories and attempted to resume operations were: 1, C. H. Merritt & Son ; 2, White, Tweedy & Smyth ; 3, W. Beckerle & Co. ; 4, John W. Green ; 5, D. E. Lowe & Co.; 6, T. Brothwell & Co. ; 7, E. A. Mallory & Sons ; and 8, T. C. Millard & Co. Several of the firms started work in some departments, and all agree that they will be running in all departments next week."

"$900 FOR ONE MUSHROOM.

" AN AMATEUR GROWER RECOUNTS HIS COSTLY EXPERIENCE.

" ' What do you say to a little roast duck and apple sauce ? ' Jones asked of a reporter, looking
over the bill of fare after they had seated themselves in the restaurant.

" ' Too rich,' the reporter answered. 'Why not
beefsteak and mushrooms ? '

" ' Anything but mushrooms ! ' Jones exclaimed.
' The last one I ate cost me something over $900,
and I 'm under a .   .   . ' "

" .   .   . near the east shore.   He has recovered
nine bodies from Cayuga Lake and as many more
from Seneca Lake."

" Last week I found nine coveys of chickens
within a half-mile of each other.   On an eighteen-
mile drive I .   .   . "

" .   .   . any Warren Street school-boy can solve.
You have a divisor, quotient, and remainder, now
find the dividend—that fish measures exactly 9 ft.
in length."

" .   .   . dashed over an old log.   The bait
was no sooner out of sight than it was caught and I
landed a 9-in. trout.   Then I began to think how I
could carry them all home and .   .   . "

" .   .   . neighborhood had skinned out the
pheasants very materially ; in fact Mr. Crawford

10

told us that he had killed only the day before nine pheasants over the same grounds that we hunted, and we only got four . . ."

"Yesterday a fisherman caught nine bass in a forenoon's fishing on Ballast Reef, and the news was quickly circulated among the disappointed visitors, with the result of inducing several of them to stay over another day to . . . "

" . . . the 'bar,' as the strip of sand known as Fire Island is called. Mr. William Ryan landed a nine-pounder the other day while trolling near the light-house. Mr. Ryan is very fond of fast horses, and is one of the most expert . . . "

"Two peddlers met in front of a nine-story tenement-house in New York. 'How is business, Aaron?'—'Very good, indeed. And how is it with you?'—'A woman just called me from the top story of this tenement. I . . . "

" . . . that Jocko Lake furnishes unusually good fishing. Sometimes a single line is rigged with nine hooks, and, if left down a short time when the trout are biting freely, will often secure nine trout, or a fish on each hook, at a single time."

"Hol' Joe he 'll come any place where dere be some folkses, he 'll beegin holler, 'Any one man want see nine rattlin snake, for twenty-fav cen', jomp on de woggin.'

"Den w'en you 'll gat on for look, hol' Joe he 'll stroke it . . . "

" ' If you will come with me about a mile out in the country, I will introduce you to the widow Sneider, now an old lady. The widow Sneider will tell you that on one morning she counted 900 (nine hundred) wagon-loads of bullheads on their way from the geyser below the dam.' "

" Mack turned to the bottom of the boat, where the three fish lay—a big old hook-jaw and two small ones, and picked up the smallest, rinsed him till he glistened, and hung him in the air—about 9 in. of trout. Then a howl of derision went up and they put on exhibition a string of . . . "

" MR. ROBERTS—I do not think the winninish and land-locked salmon are the same by any means. Why is it we never get the winninish any larger? We get the salmon weighing 25 lbs., but the winninish never weigh over 5 lbs.

" MR. BRACKETT—I have seen them weighing 9 lbs."

" From Pueblo the report says that nine men have been killed, while the operator at Rouse Junction places the number at five, and this is confirmed by the manager of a mine at Rouse ; while Trinidad states that only one man, a Deputy Sheriff, was slain. Everything favors the death of at least nine men . . ."

" Our wood-sawyer Willis, whose testimony differs from all others, has, notwithstanding his lack of adherents, much better proof of his position, for, when questioned, he not only affirmed that 'th' jays tote "trash" nine times ev'ry Friday t' make th' fire hotter to burn up we's souls with, in the "Bad Place," ' but that he has actually seen them engaged in the business."

EN KLAPJAGT PAA DANSKE FJELDE.

THE gray haze of a November morning made a monochrome with the gray walls and paved streets of Denmark's capital, as Dr. Warming and I with our guns and canvas suits and big boots, stepped into our carriage in Vesterbrogade and rattled off past the early milkman with his bumping, thumping cans, and past the homeward-bound gambler, who was damp and limp from long exposure to night air.

Uncas, the setter, we had left whining and barking and pawing at the door, and my heart went out in pity for the poor fellow as my mind reverted to earlier days and a little red school-house beneath the butternut trees in a small Connecticut village. A loose clap-boarded, lichen-

blotched school-house in which I myself
could have whined and barked and pawed
at the door when the gentians by the
brookside were nodding toward the muskrat tracks in the sand, and when the
ruffed grouse in freedom walked and flew
whither they would in the gay-colored
breezy autumn forest. Yes! I could sym-
pathize with Uncas now. We were going
on a drive hunt, and knew that the ambi-
tious setter could not resist the temptation
to follow if a sleek-limbed hare should
shake its tail in his face and challenge him
for a run. I had hunted deer in the Royal
Forest, had shot partridges on the private
estates of wealthy landowners, and in fact
had enjoyed every luxury in the way of
shooting that my Danish friends could
furnish, with the exception of the drive
hunt which had been arranged for the
day of which I write.

We reached the suburbs of Copenhagen
and smelled the rich salt air from the
reedy marshes just as the haze in the east
began to grow coppery, and the peeps of
the small birds fluttering from the hedges

by the wayside told of the beginning of their day. Flocks of sparrows were already feeding in the stubble, and their chirrups sounded clear and loud through the crisp morning air. The white frost on the fences sparkled on the eastern side of the way, and the heavy-framed laborers with wooden shoes, carrying agricultural implements on their shoulders, bowed politely to us as they passed on their way to work. Broad meadows stretched out to the right and to the left. Fields of yellow wheat stubble, of green and gray turnips, and of red cabbage dotted the hillsides. Here and there stood a dark Norway spruce tree or a clump of beech trees. The air felt just as Pennsylvania air feels, and the groups of apple and pear and cherry trees might just as well have been standing in somebody's back yard in Massachusetts; but nevertheless there was a something different, an indescribable foreignness about the scenery which impressed me constantly and pleasantly.

My enthusiastic companion, who spoke no English, and whom I constantly admonished to speak slowly, would start off on an enraptured strain about prospects every few minutes, in the same way as Sam and I encourage each other when the ruffed grouse at home are fat and the chestnuts shine in plump brownness through the yellow and crumply leaves under foot. Thistles and plantain and clover grew with familiar grasses along the road, and shocks of corn were waiting to be husked. A little way ahead a high thatched windmill swung its long arms slowly around in the light breeze, and over the top of a hill to the right the ends of another windmill's arms appeared and disappeared at regular intervals. Every now and then a big white and black magpie slid from a tree overhead as we jogged along, or a flock of lead-colored crows (*Corvus cornix*) changed fence-posts and cawed a recognition. Over the bay long lines of geese were cleaving the air with waving wings, and an occasional mallard or snipe settled in among the feathery-topped rushes near us.

The sun was beginning to soften the

air of the perfect autumn morning when
we espied the group of jolly Danes who
were waiting at the place of rendezvous.
There were Ole Larsen and Lars Olesen,
and Neils Holmsen and Holm Nielsen,
and Asmus Rasmussen and Rasmus As-
mussen, and Ask Bjoerken, and Axel Ha-
gerup, and Olof Qvist, Hjelt Raavad, and
Sell Maag, and Hjalmer Bjoernsen, and a
lot of others whose names have in some
unaccountable way slipped my mind.

Twenty or thirty flaxen-haired, strong-
waisted boys wearing home-made clothes
and heavy wooden shoes, carried wooden
clappers and old tin pans and other racket-
producing implements. The noise part
of the hunt was to be left to the responsi-
bility of the boys, and never was respon-
sibility carried more lightly. There were
hunting suits of corduroy, and hunting
suits of canvas, and hunting suits of
business suits there. There were English guns with shoulder-straps, and Belgian
guns with shoulder-straps, and American
guns with shoulder-straps : and all these
straps wrinkled the coats of their respective

owners as the hunters stood about chatting in Danish and preparing for the start. Many of the men could speak German and French, and it was surprising to find that many who had had little opportunity to speak English were able to carry on conversation in that tongue.

A few minutes were spent in making arrangements, and then we formed in a line out across the fields, the hunters about two gunshots apart and the boys sandwiched in between. There we stood in picturesque style, the fox-tail grass and and the red-flowered wild poppies and the seedy pig weeds glistening about our feet with melting frost, while every one impatiently awaited the signal to start. Suddenly a bugle blast rang out along the line, and at the same instant the boys began a lively clapping and clattering, and the shooters shouted in glee to each other, as with cocked guns and accelerated heartbeats we began a military march toward the horizon.

From under the very feet of Stjerne on my left an enormous hare bounds out like a mule struck by a locomotive, and with ears laid back and short tail bobbing begins to measure off the ground in rods. A No. 10 roar calls out for him to halt, and through the smoke we see the hare tumbling and rolling and kicking sand and grass into the air. A boy runs forward, and grabbing the heavy animal by its hind legs throws it over his shoulder and hurries back to the line. A hare weighs as much as a shotgun, but no boy ever felt too tired to carry one of them. Another flash further down the line, and another an instant later, excite the boys to the development of a tin pandemonium.

There goes a hare which was not hit and three dogs start after him at once. Over the meadow they go at a tremendous rate, the hare hardly touching the ground with his feet, but in a brown and white line of waving motion leading the canines easily. Were he to keep straight on at this rate he would be in Moscow in time for luncheon, but playful in his fleetness he turns, and circling back runs almost up to Hvide, who strikes him in the fore quarter

with a stray shot. Off he scurries, handi-
capped, with one of the dogs close at his
heels; but it seems as though a bar of
steel prevented the dog from gaining the
last necessary foot of distance, while the
hare bounds up and down so fast that I
wonder why he does n't shake his head off
or fray the end of his tail. Hares are put
together with strings, and this one does
not even shake an ear loose. The shooters
hold their breaths in their intense interest. Suddenly the hare doubles, and
the dog in the funniest kind of a way
goes sprawling several yards past before
he can acquire the saw-horse stiff-legged-
ness which he requires for stopping. Another dog springs open-mouthed on the
hare, but he opens his mouth too widely
or something of the sort, because the hare
seemed to pop right through him and
come out smiling. The third dog joins the
first one, and together they dash furiously
through the grass and out across the
ploughed field. The hare misses his
footing and a gleam of white belly fur
appears for an instant as he rolls on a

furrow. The dogs make a dive for him, but they are too simultaneous and stand themselves up like three muskets on an armory floor. The hare has all of the room and time that he wants, and leaves the dogs standing as pigeon-toed and discouraged as a man with a broken collar-button on a hot evening at the theater. A puff of smoke and a loud bang are followed by a reaping of grass leaves about the hare, and the dogs have an opportunity to " quit their fooling." It seems as much a pity to let off that hare's energy as it does to waste the steam from an engine at the end of a day's work.

As we start on again Bjoernstjerne quickly jumps around and fires into the turnip leaves through which we have just passed, bagging a hare and half a dozen turnips, but letting a boy get off as a fast driver to the right without hitting him. Notwithstanding the noise and disturbance the hare had lain so close that he was passed unobserved and might have escaped if he had allowed us to do the departing instead of trying to do part of it himself. Division of labor has its disadvantages. Ploughed land seems to be the best for hares, and every few minutes one goes bounding out from a furrow and vaulting from one hummock to another. Occasionally one will jump wild but the dogs usually manage to get him back to one of the hunters. All at once the clappers stop their racket and every one looks to see what game is coming. A couple of big wood-pigeons are bearing for us bow on. Nearer they come and larger they grow, until it is too late for them to pass—put their tails as hard to port as they may. Their white-lined wings go with misty speed and they spring away from each other overhead. Three or four guns belch forth rolling volumes of smoke, and the hurtling storm of lead perforates atmosphere and pigeons alike. Down come both birds together, twisting and whirling and losing downy feathers as they fall. Little straw-colored Harold runs out and brings in the biggest bird, wiping the blood from its bill with his fingers and then wiping his fingers on his

pantaloons—just as he does for his own
chubby nose. He is anxious to carry the
bird and I tell him he must be very careful
with it as I want the skin to stuff. Such
obedient carefulness as he displays one
seldom sees in a boy, and when he is
trudging through a wet spot he holds
the bird over his head where the saw-
grass won't muss it, until tripping up on
a willow root the poor little fellow snaps
shut like a jackknife and pokes the
pigeon so deep down in the mud with
one knee that the saw-grass turns green
with envy.

Here comes a short-eared owl from the
marsh. Swinging along with soft noiseless flip flops he skims the perfumed air
from the aster tops, and carelessly wafts
himself into our dangerous midst. The
opportunity is too good an one for Sven-
sen to resist.

The clappers are again quiet as a mallard duck flying high passes over the line
on his way to some small inland pond which
he knows about. Half a pound of shot
goes up after him, but he points his bill

toward the heavens and winnows the air
finer than ever with his stout whistling
pinions. Hardly has the smoke stopped
sifting through the poplar sprouts ahead
before a pair of pretty little blue doves
dart past like arrows. One, two, three
shots and one dove is down ; four, five,
six, seven shots and the second one
tumbles into the clover. How smooth
their feathers are, and what delicately
moulded heads and dainty red feet they
have !

"Smukke dove ! Saa lille og nydelig,"
says big Waldemar, as he brings one in
in his hand.

It does n't take long for the sun to
reach the noon-mark in Danish November,
and it gets there before one really feels
that Phœbus dare stand up straight. A
wagon which has been following us slowly
through the meadows now drives up and
the hunters and boys brush each others'
ears with their elbows as they help themselves to the cheese and beer and boiled
eggs, and other luxuries which the wagon
contains.

A small ravine, on the grassy banks of
which Vikings probably sat on grasshop-
pers and sharp stones just as we do
to-day, runs through the fields near
our halting place. We pull the crooked,
stiff hares out straight, smooth their
fur, and lay them in heaps by our sides.
We toss lunch tidbits to the dogs, light
pipes and cigars, kick our heels into
the sod, throw egg-shells at the boys,
and joke and laugh until the uneasy
members of the party suggest that we be
off again. The dogs notice the first
movement, and in exuberant spirits leap
over their masters, and over each other,
and bark in good plain English. This time
the line of march extends down towards
the sea. More hares spring up and die,
ephemerally. Another short-eared owl
and another pair of doves find that our
influence was more reaching than they had
thought. We are approaching a series of
sand knolls which are covered with tall,
dry, sparsely growing grass. The clappers remain quiet. A word of caution is
passed along the line.

Hardly have our feet begun to crunch the loose sand when a covey of twenty partridges bursts out of the grass with an explosive rush of wings, and spreading their ruddy tails widely, and crying *quirlp-quirlp, quirlp-quirlp,* in shrill, quail-like tones, they lengthen out into a straggling flock and head for the marsh. Poulsen, who is nearest to the birds, coolly stops one of them with each barrel, but Iversen, who tries to kill the whole bevy at once, fails to get any of it. Two men off on the left pick out four passing birds, and the rest of the partridges, after a rapid flight of a few hundred yards, sail off on curved wings and scatter singly among the tussocks of grass. A bird which stayed behind flies up almost at my feet with a startling whirr, but he joins the minor part of the flock. The scattered patridges lie in a territory which belongs to a distant part of our line.

The sand knolls crossed, we reach the marsh, but on we go through the sloppy reeds and splashy grass holes as though we were on a board floor. In goes little

Ivan just ahead of me, splattering the water with his heavy shoes, and sprinkling it over his fox-skin cap and home-made blue blouse. In go Bjoerken and Jansen and Raavad. Out go a snipe and a fox and a duck. Snipe jump up on all sides and zig-zag off "skaiching" huskily, just as they do when Culver and I flush them from the rich juicy ground of a sweet New Jersey swamp.

The marshes here look very much like our own marshes at home, and any one not a botanist would have difficulty in determining from the surroundings whether he were in New Jersey or in this far north Sjaelland. The ducks are rather wild and they usually manage to get out of the way of our noisy party before we get within range of them. Now and then a single mallard will lie concealed under the fallen sedge until we are close upon him, and then with loud quacks and swishing wings he tries to escape.

The daylight is fading rapidly and by four o'clock it will be too dark to shoot. Working back toward the hills in broken line we pass the house of a peasant family and my friend Dr. Warming and I stop for a moment to see the place. The one-story house with whitewashed stone and mortar walls is built to surround a square court-yard. A single large gateway leads through the south wall of the building into this court, in the middle of which latter a high wooden pump is surrounded by ducks and geese and chickens. The court is cobble-stoned, and pretty green mosses run off along the damp crevices between the stones. Several doors open into this central yard. The few small windows are set deeply in the walls of the house. The high-peaked roof of two-foot-thick straw thatching is covered with broad patches of rich green moss. Part of the house is the barn, and the horses, cows, wagons, poultry and family all go and come through the opening in the south wall of the building. Two or three dark Norway spruce trees spread their bottle-green branches over the house, and the contrast with the whitewashed walls is a striking one. Several lead-colored crows flew up on the thirty-foot-high straw stack by the barn as we approached, and they now sat cawing at us within easy stone shot.

We are greeted by the children, who pull off their caps politely and then rattle their wooden shoes on the cobbles as they run off to their mammas in the doorways. Strong, handsome, yellow-haired children, with bright faces and clear gray eyes. I looked in at a school window one day and the whole room seemed to be lighted up with a mellow glow of yellow hair. All Danish children have to be strong. The weak ones die off when they try to learn the language, and like Connecticut River shad, only the most robust are able to surmount the difficulties which beset their way.

Doctor and I, on invitation, step into a simply-furnished room, with white-sanded floor, and sit down by the square table in straight-backed chairs. Our host is delighted when he hears that I am a Yankee, and he wishes to bring out the household penates in bottles. Turning to little Maren, who stands bashfully covering up two-thirds of her grin with a fold of her mother's dress, I say in my most enticing Danish, "Kom him lille pige, og sit paa mit knae. Jeg skal ikke gjoere dig ondt." But my pronunciation gives her a terrible fright, and, disappearing from sight in the dress like a young kangaroo in its mamma's waist, she begins to sob. A looking-glass hangs on the wall, together with two or three highly colored lithographs representing "The Girl of the Period," "The Old Oaken Bucket" and "The Pleasures of the Country," etc. Several mottoes worked on perforated paper with bright-colored worsted are stuck up here and there, but one can't read the words any better than he can read the same in worsted English. I guess likely they say "God bless our home," and things like that. A large Jerome clock stands on top of the unpainted cupboard in one corner of the room, and from poles overhead are hung dried herbs. A wooden bracket by the looking-glass holds the usual comb, which needs false teeth, and the loose-backed hair brush, which has spanked some boy too hard.

It is time to go. As I step to the stone threshold, the lord of the manor extends a hand like the hand of Providence, and engulfing my own in a maelstrom of fingers, he works my arm up and down in the same manner as he does an eight-foot pump-handle out in the court. I escape in fairly good condition, however, and amid profuse good-byes we go out through the big gate and into the field of tall, curly-leaved green cabbage to join the straggling hunters who are preparing a line for one more trip across the fields.

All is ready, and together we advance in imposing array, each man anxious to add just a little more game to his list. Every few minutes a big hare makes a sudden spurt, and tries to kick the world around faster on its axis, but he is stopped in time to save the time of day. A flock of partridges make the trembling dry grass wave in little swirls, as the birds, with a mighty spring, launch out into the air right near us. Glass-ball shooters would have instinctively yelled out "broke" if they had seen the feathers start when four or five of the birds suddenly became noiseless in mid-air.

It is almost dark when we reach the road and take a short cut for the old inn of Valdby Kro. A fox runs out into the field in the distance, and I make every one laugh by my pronunciation of his Danish name "raev." They say that the word which I use sounds like the Danish name for a boot target. Two or three of us try to scramble over the rickety fence at the back of the inn, but a sample dog, —a Great Dane,—is waiting for us on the other side, and as my friend says that it hurts to have a leg pulled off by a dog of this size, we decide to disappoint the dog, and let him wait for somebody else. I don't care how prosperous a hotel may be, it is bad policy for the landlord to keep a dog which destroys customers before they have paid any bills. Inside the hotel guns are stacked and hung up in the reception room, and hats and heavy coats follow suit. Over in one corner is a great heap

of hares, boys, birds, and dogs. Every-
one is happy, and securely seated with
his glass of lager—of cool, cream-foamed
lager which trickles over the edge of the
mug, and mingles with the misty con-
densed moisture on the outside—is telling
his neighbor confidentially just how it
was that he had the good luck to kill most
of the game bagged during the day.

A smile born of light hearts and lighter
stomachs seems to flash across the room
when the dining-room bell gives the signal for the shuffling of heavy boots to
commence. The tables are creaking with
solid sections of brown, juicy, steaming
roasts, and piles of mealy potatoes envel-
oped in hot fog, and long white platters of
whole salmon through whose tender torn
skin the pink flakes and streaks of white
fat look all ready for the limpid golden
butter-sauce which stands in the brimming
full dishes near by. Tall handsome Danish girls are running hither and thither with
chicken soup for this man, and hare soup
for that man, and extricating order from
the chaos on the table with a marvellous

degree of skill. Good nature is rampant, and the fast delivered hearty speeches are followed by rousing echoing cheers. Cries of "skol ! skol !" follow every toast in which the Yankee is mentioned, with a vigor which shows how deep and real their feelings of hospitality are, and men come from the distant tables to express friendly sentiments toward America and Americans in general.

An hour passes by, and the tide of speech gradually subsides. The stage of quiet enjoyment is ushered in with the blue-flaming plum-pudding ; and coffee with cream melts all dispositions into one easy flowing current of serene contentment. Snatches of Danish song which have been idly travelling about the table for several minutes, begin to join forces as we light fragrant cigars and pipes, and lean back lazily and stretchful in our chairs.

While others sing, I pull from my hunting coat-pocket the old battered meerschaum, and fill it with yellow, fragile grained "Lone Jack." That dear old meerschaum that I have smoked by my campfire in the Adirondack forest, while the birch log sizzled and snapped, and fitful gleams of red flame lighted up the form of the strong antlered buck which was drawn up on the moss by my side.

The same fond pipe that I have smoked in the evening light while I sat with Sam on the threshold of a Pennsylvania farmhouse, and the October breeze whirled the dead leaves about our day's load of ruffed grouse, woodcock, and quail, and toyed with the wavy locks of our tired and sleepy setters.

The same beloved meerschaum that I have smoked on a Connecticut June noontime in a sunny, ferny corner of the rail fence among the white birches, where the fresh growing grass on the bank stirred shadows into the clear waters of Poohtatook Brook with every zephyr, and the brown thrush in the willow-top asked the buttercup-dancing, air-prancing, soul-entrancing bobolink to call me away from my reverie.

The same quieting pipe that I have

smoked in the midwinter icy blast in Great South Bay, while the staunch sloop plunged and strained at her anchor among the rushing, voice-smothering, white-capped waves, while the wind whistled and hissed through the rigging, the boom creaked and swung with every lurch, and the heap of ducks exchanged places with the bushel of oysters on the cabin floor. While the thundering breakers on the outer beach, furious in the easterly gale, bellowed and groaned in hoarse monotone between the reverberations from the tons of black and whitening billows rolling in mighty front high upon the sand bulwarks, and dark night clouds, all ragged and torn, drifted low and swiftly overhead.

Every whiff of smoke from the pipe is richly flavored with the essence of old associations, but I am precipitated back into Denmark as one of the party, a gigantic, red faced, good-natured hunter, mounts a platform at one end of the dining-room, and prepares to auction off our game for the benefit of the poor people of the village. This is a customary proceeding after such a hunt as we have had, and the bidding is spirited, some of the hares bringing four or five times their market price.

The auctioneer gets one krone (twenty-seven cents) for one of his assistants whom he holds up before the audience, and a smaller man who is held out at half arm's-length by the big one, is knocked down to a bidder at ti oere (two and a half cents).

ONE DEER.

DICK and I were camping at a beautiful lake in the Adirondacks. It was rather late in the season and the deer that a few weeks previously had been in the habit of coming to the edges of the streams and lakes to nip the lily-buds and wade about in the shallow water, were seldom seen. Occasionally an old buck would come out at evening and take a stroll along the sandy margin of the lake, adding for the moment a touch of wilder beauty to the dark forest background, and after standing proudly at some rocky point and surveying the scene, would disappear again into the woods.

A small bay half way up the lake seemed to be a favorite place for the, deer as innumerable tracks were always to be seen in the sand along the shore,

and one afternoon when we were almost
out of venison in camp I suggested to
Dick that it would be the proper thing
for us to make a trip in the evening to
this place.

The wood for the camp-fire was cut and
piled at a convenient distance from the
smouldering back-log all ready for a glorious blaze on our return, and just before
sundown I took my place in the bow of
our little boat with the Ballard rifle across
my knees, while Dick took the stern with
the paddle.

Long shadows were reaching out from
the big pines and hemlocks on the west
shore, the valleys were already in darkness, and the long red rays of the fast
setting sun streaming through the tree-
tops illumined the rest of the forest with
a hazy evening light. Great tree trunks
lay partly sunken in the dark clear water,
their arms reaching grimly out, and quiet
reigned over all, the paddle in Dick's
skilled hand making not the slightest
sound.

As we silently glided along, a loon far

up the lake caught sight of us, and his wild querulous call ringing through the forest was answered by echo and sent wavering from cliff to cliff. Again and again the weird cry echoed and re-echoed from the mountain sides and was sent from shore to shore, and an eagle soaring high overhead answered with its screams. The reverberations ceased, and the stillness was broken only by the song of a happy cross-bill within the short range of his little voice. A mink came swimming alongside of us, his bright mischievous eyes trying to make out what we were. Suddenly an otter's head appeared above the water, and soon another, and another, and in the most amusing way they bobbed up and down and spit at us in their spiteful way. For two or three minutes the otters swam along ahead of us, diving and appearing again, and finally they disappeared all at once, probably going to pursue their calling of catching the big trout which abounded in the lake.

Gradually we neared the little bay, and as we rounded the rocky point Dick stopped paddling. The boat glided slowly along with its own motion as we carefully scanned every fallen hemlock for a sight of red hair, and in a moment I heard a low whisper, "See that buck on the right!" at the same instant catching sight of a pair of horns behind a stump that stood quite a way out in the water, and not more than ten rods from us. The old fellow had evidently been watching us just a little longer than we had been watching him, and had taken good pains to keep his eyes over the stump and very little of the rest of his body in sight. I felt the tremor of the boat again as Dick cautiously plied the paddle, and we tried to move to a position where I could see enough to shoot at, but the buck knew what we were about, and kept backing around until he could go no further, when with five or six long bounds, with flag raised, he made for a windfall and stopped behind it for a minute, snorting and stamping, before taking his final leap into the underbrush. He stood tail toward me, with his head turned and looking over his shoulder,

supposing that he was well protected
by the branches, but there was where
he made a miscalculation, for at least a
square foot of red was in sight. Quickly
I levelled the rifle, and as the echoes rang
through the forest the buck made one
grand leap and stumbled as he struck the
ground, rolling clear over, with feet kicking wildly in the air. In an instant he
was up again and had disappeared. A
few quick strokes with the paddle toward
shore, and Dick jumped out and started
in the direction that the deer had taken,
stopping long enough to motion to me
that he found blood.

For several minutes I waited in sus-
pense. It was fast growing darker, and
the minutes were getting twice as long as
in a stopped watch, when I heard Dick
call from a point along the shore above
me. The paddle was no longer needed,
so I pulled out the oars and, getting them
into the locks, rowed as rapidly as possible toward Dick. He had tracked the
buck to the water's edge, and was just
saying that we would find him mortally

wounded along the shore somewhere,
when, with a great snapping of branches
and splashing of water, the red fellow
sprang out of a windfall into the lake and
started to swim for a little island near by.
Dick jumped into the bow, and I pulled
the oars with a vengeance, not daring to
look around, but guided by the hoarse
breathing of the panting deer as he swam.
Rapidly we neared him, and just as Dick
called out "Right oar, quick!" the boat
gave a lurch, and I knew that he had our
game by the tail. At that moment the
handles of the oars came against my ab-
domen with a jerk and pressed so hard
that I could n't catch a breath for the life
of me. "Hold up, Dick!" I gasped.
"For H-e-a-v-e-n's s-a-k-e hold up!"
The oars kept pressing so hard that I
could not get out another word, until
Dick, roaring with laughter, reached
around and threw one of the oars out of
its rowlock. In my excitement I had forgotten that Dick was not the motive
power at the bow, and that the fast
swimming buck was the cause of bring-

ing into practice a very simple problem in levers.

We had only a few yards more to go before shallow water would be reached, and picking up the rifle, I intended to stop our locomotive, but the boat was unsteady, and I fired the bullet directly into the heart of the Adirondack wilderness. Another bullet went on the same errandless mission. We were almost in the shallow water, and shutting my teeth together with a firm resolve to hold steady, I sent a bullet through the neck of the deer, and with a convulsive start he sent the spray flying in every direction, and then lay kicking upon the water.

Towing the deer to the shore, we got him into the boat, and as I took the bow again, Dick took up the paddle and we started for camp.

How fine the old buck looked in the evening light, with his white belly up and legs gracefully bent, as his head lay between my knees and I stroked his smooth ears and opened the dark eyes and patted his neck.

As we neared camp the stars were sending silvery gleams over the ripples in our wake. A glimpse of the back-log burning low showed us where to land, and the smell of the smoke hanging heavily over the water was a reminder of the comforts in store.

The boat grated on the pebbly bottom, and jumping out, we rolled out our game and dragged him the short distance to camp. Lichen-covered sticks were soon snapping and roaring on the camp-fire, and the forest around was all aglow as the sparks arose with the smoke and floated off among the branches of the trees overhead. The red embers settled in a ruddy heap, and the last piece of venison from the deer which Dick had killed a few days previously, and half a dozen big trout were pulled from the moss by the spring where we had stored them ready for use. As they broiled and browned before the birch logs the juice trickled out and fell sizzling among the coals, sending fragrant aromas in every direction. Our birch-bark plates were filled as only the rich can afford to fill them in the city. And then, in a condition of supreme contentment I leaned my back against a giant pine, crossed my feet over the buck's glossy flank and lit my pipe. Dick stretched himself out at full length upon the moss near by, and as the blue puffs floated around our heads we told of former exploits with deer and bears until the pipes and the camp-fire burned low.

A BIT OF GROUSE HUNTER'S LORE.

THE game laws of New York allow ruffed grouse shooting between the first day of September and the first day of January, and although the young birds are powerful and quite knowing early in the season, they are not much hunted until the autumn leaves are falling and the cool, invigorating air allows the hunter to climb and tramp over windfalls and rocks with comfort. During the months of September and October the young grouse have comparatively short tails and small ruffs, so that they are readily distinguished from the old birds, but by the latter end of the season many of them are in perfect feather except that they lack the sheen, like that of polished mahogany, which can be observed when the back of an old bird

is held in the proper light.   The very
large birds with iridescent black ruffs are
usually cocks, although it is frequently
difficult to find any marks of differentia-
tion .in plumage which will distinguish
them from hens, and hunters are very
often mistaken as to the sex of any particular ruffed grouse. The best test without dissection is perhaps that afforded by
spreading the tail to its full extent.   If
the two external tail feathers can be
brought into a straight line with each
other before the other feathers of the tail
separate from each other at the margins,
the possessor of that tail is in all probability a male bird.   The feathers of the
tail of the hen bird usually separate from
each other while the two external tail
feathers are making an obtuse angle.   It
is customary for hunters to suppose that
the birds with brown or chocolate-colored
ruffs are females, but the color of the ruff
is not a distinctive sex mark.

The general coloration of ruffed grouse
varies greatly in different localities, the
"partridges" from northern New Eng-

land, for instance, being almost invariably ashy gray in general effect, the color of the tail being most pronounced.   In Pennsylvania the "pheasants" give an impression of reddish brown coloring, and the tails of these birds are beautifully rich in their reddish elements.   In New York State we find red birds and gray birds in about equal numbers, and in one brood we find individuals representing both extremes in such color variation, just as is the case among the screech owls.   Ruffed grouse from Oregon and from Texas are smaller and much lighter than their Eastern relatives.   Late in the autumn the grouse develop a row of narrow movable projecting scales along the sides of the toes for aids in walking upon slippery snow and ice, and these scutellæ, as they are called, drop off when the snow melts in the spring.   The average weight of full-grown Eastern grouse is about twenty-three ounces, but this weight varies two or three ounces in accordance with the character and abundance of the food supply.   The food in the autumn includes almost all berries that are accessible in any given locality, but sumac and cedar berries are not usually eaten until winter. The grouse eat beechnuts, acorns, chestnuts, mushrooms, vetch pods and seeds, witch-hazel flowers, and many succulent leaves. They rarely touch wheat, maize, oats, or barley, but of buckwheat they are inordinately fond, and early in the season they strip off the flowers and immature grains, and continue to glean in the buckwheat fields until the stubble is deeply covered with snow.

Hunters who are familiar with the birds' habits beat the fences and deep-furrowed, plowed ground all about the buckwheat fields that are not too far removed from the woods, and find there many birds that the sportsman in the brush knows nothing about. Grouse are fond of tearing the fleshy fruit of the skunk cabbage to pieces in order to get at the seeds and pulp. They devour the fruit of all of the species of wild grapes with avidity, and a covey of grouse feeding among the tangled festoons of grape-vines furnishes an inspiriting spectacle for one who knows how to approach them with due caution. The leaves of the bishop's cap (*Tiarella cordifolia* and *T. nuda*) are as staple an article of diet with ruffed grouse as bread and butter are for the American citizen, and at all seasons of the year fragments of the rough-lobed leaves may be found in their crops ; even to the exclusion of all other articles of diet at times. During the winter the food consists principally of the buds of birch, poplar, and maple trees, the leaves and berries of the wintergreen, and the leaves of the bishop's caps ; and as there are very few days during the winter when grouse cannot find an abundance of some one of these forms of provender they are almost always in good condition and "as plump as partridges." Kalmia leaves, which are sometimes eaten by them in winter, are said on good authority to make the flesh temporarily poisonous for man, and the fact that the birds' food directly affects their flesh is exemplified in the delicious aromatic flavor of grouse that have been feeding extensively upon birch buds and wintergreens, the grateful odor pervading the whole house when such birds are so unfortunate as to get upon the hot kitchen stove just before dinner time.

Ruffed grouse are as neat in their habits as such proud and self-respecting birds ought to be, and they are very fond of dusting in the wallow holes which they make in the dry dust of crumbling logs in the woods. Wherever the grouse live we are so certain to find their dusting holes that the hunter wastes no time in the woods in which the crumbling logs have not been thus utilized by the élite. During the day the birds spend most of their time in the brushy edges of the woods and in the brambly gullies that extend out in the fields, and if there are stumps near at hand in the open, the grouse are fond of running out about them and hiding there during the middle of the day. We should naturally expect to find the grouse on the sunniest hillsides when the weather is very cold, but they seem to be rather indifferent to the temperature of their surroundings and the covey is almost as likely to be found in the dreary north-facing ravine as on the warm southern exposures. When they are in company the birds keep up a constant talking to each other, but in low voices as though fearful of being overheard. There are querulous notes from the spinsters and solemn warnings from the dignified matrons when the obstreperous young cocks challenge each other to a wrestle, but the loudest vocal expression of the ruffed grouse is the clucking and squealing of a bird that has lain long to the dog, when, running like a rabbit out from under the brush-heap, he bustles on roaring wing away through the swishing birch twigs and gives vent to his emotions as he departs. Not all grouse squeal when thus flushed, but they seldom fail to utter their loudest notes when alighting on a tree overhead after being startled ; and when running for a hiding-place they utter a hurried " *quit, quit, quit,*" that attracts the immediate attention of the dog. A mother grouse, with young, whines precisely like a dog when an enemy is near her brood.

At night the grouse usually sleep upon the ground, and indifferently in the woods or out in the open clearing if the weather is dry. When it is rainy they sleep under logs, or rocks, or clumps of conifers, and frequently a whole covey will be found at night scattered along under an old tumble-down fence in the woods. In winter when the snow is deep they sleep either high up in coniferous trees or under the snow in the open, so that just at evening it is no uncommon sight to see a covey of grouse diving from wing, one after another, into the snow. If the weather is very boister-ous and the birds happen to dive down to a patch of wintergreens or clover or young winter wheat they may remain under the snow for several days, burrowing for short distances and eating the green leaves that are thus found. When a grouse is sitting quietly at no great depth beneath the snow, a little hole about as large as one's finger is kept open by the bird's breath, and the moisture congealing in large flakes upon the frosty twigs or grass just over the hole will easily locate the bird for a good observer ; and the grouse in such a position will allow one to approach quite near before he leaves his comfortable room beneath the winds.

The snow is sometimes too hard to serve for house purposes, and then the birds may not alight upon the ground for many days at a time, but fly from the hiding tops of evergreens to the trees in which they bud at morning and at evening. On the first warm day though, when the sun has softened the snow, the boy who is following a rabbit in the warm corner of the thicket will suddenly come upon the neatest, the trimmest and the most inspiring bird track that is ever imprinted in any woods on the pure white surface of this good earth of ours. Three evenly spread toemarks in front and one short straight mark behind. One footmark just as far in advance of the previous one as that is ahead of the one before it, and all in definite order. Here the track leads around a rock ; there it goes along the whole length of that half-sunken log and then straight out through the sheep path among the hazels. No slipshod stepper ever made such marks. So clear, so well defined, so mathematical a track is indicative only of such character as belongs to the noblest of all game birds, and perhaps the boy will hear from him in a moment. No! there is where he strutted; and there are the concentric segments of circles made by the wing tips in the snow as the wise bird flew, several minutes before danger approached. His danger was not so great, though, after all, if I am familiar with that boy, for the bird that left was game for a man of sharp wit and good judgment.

Grouse are quite apt to keep each other company in small coveys until spring, except when they are much disturbed, but certain very old birds are quite content to be solitary, and they are then difficult to approach under ordinary circumstances. A wary old bird will slide quietly out of the way as soon as he hears the sportsman approaching, and it is folly to attempt to corner him, but most of the grouse run and hide when there are signs of danger, and a good pointer or setter will follow them easily to their places of concealment. A grouse will not often remain before the pointing dog for more than two or three minutes, and then he bursts forth with the startling roar that reminds one of the sudden dumping of a coal cart upon the pavement, unnerving the hunter who is not cool and steady in his aim. If the bird makes a high flight at first he may be expected to alight upon the ground on descending. If he goes off low he will probably slant upward at the end of his flight of a few hundred yards and alight in a tree, barring accidents which are liable to happen at the hands of the gunners.

Grouse are sometimes caught in snares that are set for them on their feeding-grounds, and hunters who cannot kill a flying bird are not beneath chasing them with spaniels which bark at the flushed birds and cause them to stop, out of curiosity, and alight on limbs overhead in order to watch the antics of the dogs. The hunter can then approach closely before attracting the attention of the preoccupied grouse. It is a very difficult matter to see a grouse that has alighted in a large tree at the end of a deliberate flight, as he usually sits bolt upright very close to the trunk and moves not a feather, and unless one scans every foot of the tree systematically the bird will probably not be discovered. Hunters often declare that they have never been able to find a grouse in a tree, just as we hear young women complain that they cannot discover a four-leafed clover, and yet certain eyes are very expert at detecting grouse in trees and four-leafed clovers in the greensward ; much to the discomfiture of untrained observers who were not previously aware of their lack of the requisite power.

Wing-shooting is the most certain and the most satisfactory way of getting a good bag of grouse, and for this purpose well broken pointers or setters are indispensable. Their keen noses enable them to detect the scent of a bird that has walked along the ground perhaps half an hour previously, and they follow the trail until the vicinity of the game is reached. The bird being located in his hiding-place,

the dog stands silently pointing until the
hunter has found a good place from which
to shoot when the grouse springs out on
wing.   The most successful shots in the
brush are not often the men who make
good scores in open field shooting, for in
the latter sort of work one learns to take
sight along the barrel of his gun, and in
the woods such sighting is naturally in-
terfered with.   The best grouse hunters
of my acquaintance shoot with both eyes
open and head erect, moving the gun with
the same intuition that guides the bat-
ter in striking a ball after "suppressing
the image" of everything except that of
the object aimed at.   The image of
branches and trees upon the retina of the
eye being suppressed at will by the hunter,
he is then conscious only of the presence
of the swiftly moving bird, and this object he follows as accurately with the
gun as he would with his finger if he were
pointing out the bird to a friend.

Very nice calculations are required in
order to hit the bird, however, for if the
gun were aimed directly at a crossing

grouse at the instant of firing, the charge of shot would pass far to the rear of the game. It is necessary to know approximately the length of time required for combustion of the powder, the time occupied by the charge of shot in reaching any given point, and to judge correctly of the distance and direction of the angles and curves of flight of the bird. All of the factors excepting the first vary with each fraction of a second after the bird is on wing, so it would seem almost impossible that any one could be capable of making the calculations requisite for striking a swift-speeding grouse among the trees were it not for the aid of that peculiar faculty of instinctive co-ordination in action of brain and muscle. A strong bird is not easily killed even when fairly hit, and it seemed cruel to allow a wounded grouse to escape, but men who have been struck with shot testify that the benumbing effect was such that they did not suffer any real pain after the receipt of the injury. When we know what a fox or hawk would do with a captured grouse it makes the hunter's conscience easy.

TROUT IN A THUNDER-STORM.

ONE day in the summer of 1880, Charley and I, with our guide, Dick Crego, left our camp on Fourth Lake, for a day's trout-fishing in the south branch of Moose River. It was one of those days in July when the dweller in the city would ponder over the question in his philosophical mind as to whether life was worth living or not and decide in the negative, but in the woods the fragrant breaths from hemlocks and cool air waves from the moss-covered and ferny ground gave one an exhilaration and exuberant delight in mere existence.

The day was not a perfect one for trout-fishing, but for us lovers of nature the summer stillness of the deep forest possessed such an enchantment that the prospect of a light creel at evening had no effect on our spirits. Trout were abundant anyway, and we were catching enough every day for camp use.

As Dick quietly paddled us near the spring holes we could see the trout lazily poising themselves on their red and white marginal fins, and slightly stirring the sandy bottom with slow sweeps of their mottled tails, not caring to exert themselves to make a move for the flies which we seductively cast near them.

Once in a while under the low hanging branches of a hemlock or bunch of alders we would find a trout that was anxious to have a pull at the fly, but on the whole we had taken very few up to the middle of the afternoon, when ominous mutterings began to be heard in the south. Great thunder-heads of dark cumulus appeared over the tall pines and hemlocks and rapidly rolled toward us. The forest was wrapped in an awful stillness. Not a sound could be heard near us save an occasional muffled murmur of the water as it whirled in an eddy under some fallen tree trunk.

We had arrived at the " big spring hole " and as Dick cautiously sent the light boat close to the bank Charley and I stepped out, and bending low behind the bushes crept to an open place where we could cast our flies easily. Charley made the first cast. His flies had hardly made a ripple on the water when splash! down went his red ibis. His light rod bent into a half circle, and as I cast a quick glance at the spot I saw half a dozen trout gliding about near his hooked one with the restless eager movements which always mean hunger. My flies alighted instantly in the same place, and down went my stretcher fly with a whirl. As that trout made a quick turn I saw another calmly fasten himself on one of the dropper flies. We led our trout to one side of the pool and Dick slipped a landing net under them and threw them, tumbling and squirming, upon the grass. In a moment we had both made another cast and hooked our fish, and the rest of the trout in the eddy were excited and angry because they had not snatched the flies first.

Meanwhile the forest had grown darker and darker. The great banks of inky black clouds were low over our heads. Quivering flashes of lightning lighted up the mountains, and the heavy thunder shook the very ground and reverberated and echoed.

Cast after cast we made, and the trout seemed invigorated by the rigor of the elements. Big lusty fellows made the spray fly as they plunged after our flies with might and main. Some in their eagerness dashed clear over the flies and turned double somersaults in the air. At almost every cast a trout was hooked, and a sight of our bent rods and whirring reels would have made the Sphinx arise and whoop for joy just for once.

A gale rushed through the tops of the pines, and as they bent before the blast and the wind soughed through their branches the big drops began to fall. Still we fished until Dick fairly dragged us to the boat, which he had pulled up on

the bank and turned over. Under the
boat we crawled, and the trout flapped
about in the wet grass near us, while
lightning flashed and thunder roared.
Who says that trout will not bite in a
thunder-storm ?

COOT SHOOTING IN NEW ENGLAND.

NEW YORK, Oct. 12.

IN a recent number of *Forest and Stream* "M. H. Able" asks if the "coots" which the Eastern gunners works so hard to get are the same as the mud-hens of the Western States. One day's shooting in line would convince our friend that he was not shooting mud-hens, but that big, sturdy sea-ducks, worthy of his lead, were carrying off ounces of his Number 4 shot. The ducks which are called coots along the coast consist of three or four species. The male surf-ducks are called skunkhead coots, and their wives and yearlings gray coots. The velvet scoter is known as the white-winged coot, and the American scoter is the butter-billed coot. The eiders, also, are dragged into the "genus coot." In no sort of shooting do hunters ever get aroused to so high a pitch of excitement as while gunning for these heavy sea-ducks. The birds are abundant and are constantly on the move from one feeding-ground to another. The fresh ocean breezes key the hunters up to the last degree of manly vigor, and as the light boats ride the long swells as gracefully as a swallow floats through the air, the boom and roar of the surf among the rocks on the shore inspires the gunners with its freedom. The boats are swinging on their long anchor-lines twenty rods apart; the ducks are flying swiftly through between the boats, and every moment the heavy ten-bores are ringing out loud and clear, and the puffs of thick smoke are borne rapidly away on the breeze. Here a white-wing, the leader of the flock, struck with the Number 4s, halts and falters and plunges headlong into the waves; there a skunkhead, proud in his speed, wilts suddenly high in the air—down, down, down he comes, and the spray flies in every direction as he surges heavily into the water, while a few feathers float back on the breeze. Men are shouting, ten-bores booming ; wings are whistling, feathers flying ; coots are splashing, bounding, diving—while the rush and the roar of the breakers in the rocks keep time to the riding of the boats.

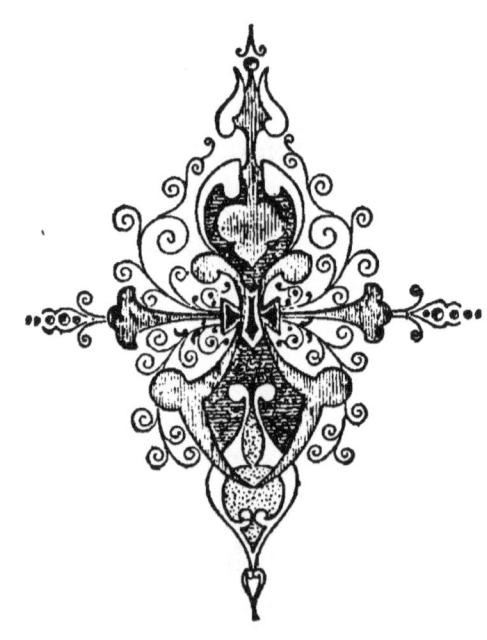

RUFFED GROUSE AMONG THE GRAPE-VINES.

SAM and I had been hunting ruffed grouse every day for a week, and Sunday had finally brought us to a halt to rest for the week ahead. It was a glorious Sabbath in a little quaint village in Wayne County, Pa. We sat on the stone slab at the kitchen door of the old farmhouse, and smoked our pipes in contentment, watching the yellow leaves as they lazily zig-zagged down to the ground from the limbs of the half bare maples, and the antiopa butterflies slowy flitting from one decayed apple to another under the trees in the orchard close by. A blue dove on the eaves of the barn cooed occasionally in a quiet, Sunday way as he basked in the November sunshine, and the hens were dozing in the holes where they had been dusting themselves an hour before, in front of the barn door. Belle and Carrie were curled up in the grass near us, dreaming of grouse that never flushed wild ; and everything was still. The sound of the church-bell down in the village seemed mellowed as though in harmony with the color of the beech and maple woods through which its vibrations reached us.

"Sam !" said I, "those grouse down by the rock cut will be in the frost grapes this morning, and I 'm going down across the lot to see if I can get near them. Don't let the dogs follow me."

The dry leaves, a foot deep, along the fence by the grape-vines seemed to rustle louder than they ever did before, as I cautiously climbed over the rails, but no grouse was near to be frightened, and although expecting the sudden dash and whirr every moment, I got near to the farther side of the little patch of vines without starting a bird, and sitting down in the leaves with my back against a mossy boulder, tried to fit it well, and

waited.   In a few minutes there was a
pattering of very light footsteps in the
leaves back of me.   Nearer and nearer
they came, stopping for a second and then
proceeding again, coming my way all of
the while.   Suddenly a surprised " peet "
on the right caused me to slowly turn my
eyes in that direction, and there, within
six feet, was a splendid male grouse, with
crest erect and tail partially spread, looking curiously at me. I kept stiller than any
little mouse, and the grouse satisfied himself that I was harmless.   He came a few
steps nearer, clucking all of the while, and
mounting a stone, spread his tail to its
fullest extent, and with crest and tail erect,
with ruff displayed, and with wings drooping to his feet, he turned two or three
times around, like a turkey gobbler.
Then composing himself again he took
another good look and walked around in
front.

At that moment another grouse, a
younger one, had come around the rock
by which I was sitting, and he too went
through the same performance, but not in

such fine style. Both birds then walked on a way, watching me all of the while, and soon four more grouse came in sight. They walked within three rods, but paid me no attention, and busied themselves picking up fallen frost grapes. Suddenly there was a rush overhead and a grouse alighted in the vines just above me and commenced picking at a bunch of grapes, his smooth plumage with the dark markings on the sides seeming more beautiful than anything I had ever seen. Once in a while he looked down at me over his shoulder, erected his crest, and gave an interested " peet, peet," and then went on picking grapes again.

In a short time eleven grouse were in sight, moving about as gracefully as could be, putting their little feet lightly down on the dead leaves, and all engaged in hunting for food. One of them flew up to the one already in the vines, and then nearly all followed, and commenced picking the grapes that hung in scattered clusters.

All of this while I had remained perfectly

quiet, but my position was fast becoming uncomfortable. An edge of rock was boring into the middle of my back ; another sharp piece had done its level best to penetrate the back of my head, and a jagged stump had worked just as far into my leg as it could possibly get, so that I had to move. The grouse all seemed alarmed at the sight. They sat straight and motionless among the vines, but none flew. For several minutes they remained in this position, and knowing that I was discovered I arose, expecting to see all of them dart off at once. This they did not do, however, but started slowly one at a time, and sailed off only a few rods into the woods.

14

WING SHOOTING VERSUS GROUND SHOOTING.

NEW YORK, Jan. 21st.

Editor Forest and Stream:

This controversy as to whether it is proper to shoot a sitting grouse or not will probably never be brought to an end. I am acquainted with a great many men who would scorn to shoot a quail or woodcock, if the bird was not upon the wing; but who would not hesitate to shoot a grouse upon the ground. On the the other hand, I know sportsmen to whom a grouse so killed would be an albatross about the neck.

A certain number of men will never consent to lose caste by shooting any game bird that is not flying, while others will allow their color-line to shade off into the dusky by making an exception of the ruffed grouse.

Then there are the boys to be considered. How well do I remember the joyous days of childhood when most of my hours were spent in the woods, and when the birds, and animals, and fishes, and plants seemed to be the only things in the whole world worthy of any consideration.

I knew just where to find the old partridge's nest in early May on the warm sunny hillside among the sprouts and junipers. How often I have watched the mother bird on her nest ; and when she skurried away I would stretch myself at full length by her treasures, and with my head between my little hands would gaze eagerly at the eight or ten buff-colored eggs and ponder over their contents, and think of what they would bring forth. When my visits to the nest were frequent, I used to imagine that the old bird grew tamer, and that she knew better than to be afraid.

After the little downy chicks were hatched I could always find the brood. If they were not down by the spring brook, where the fox-grapes and hellebores grew, they were up along the old fence among the cedars and cat-briers, or they were in the pastures among the huckleberry bushes. At any rate, they had favorite resorts, and I always knew where those resorts were.

When the autumn days drew near and the birds had grown, I used to lug out the old gun, and, while hunting lesser game, my heart would beat fast as I penetrated the haunts of the partridges. The old gun was long and heavy, and it balanced like an armful of oars ; and I was too little and too anxious to be steady.

When after much patient watching I happened to see one of my patridges upon the ground before he flew, I nervously set the ponderous hammer back, and poking the long barrel through the tangling branches, and trembling more than I ever have since in the presence of much larger game, I would pull hurriedly on the trigger.

Why would n't that trigger hurry up ? I could feel it pull, and pull, and pull, and then my small finger would take a fresh grip and draw with a vengeance, and through the smoke from the explosion I could see the bird go whirring away with no part of him blasted.

Later in the season I used to set twitch-ups for the rabbits, and steel-traps for muskrats, and snares for the partridges. How anxiously and how often I would visit those snares, and every time that I approached them, with bated breath I peered through the bushes to see if there was "one in." When from a distance, part of the snare fence could be seen all knocked out of shape and the dried leaves scattered about in confusion, I would eagerly jump to the dead partridge that lay in their midst, and pulling from his neck the coil he could not shuffle off, I would take the bird in my lap and stroke his feathers one by one, spread his feet out in my hand, and rub his soft breast against my cheek. It seemed to be too good to be true ; life was overflowing with happiness. The robins and red squirrels and other standard boys' game would fade into insignificance for the time being, and the partridge brought a pleasure keener than some mortals seem to experience.

But years have rolled by, and the snare and the old single-barrel are things of the past. I have owned many a fine gun and hunted many a fine setter or pointer in far distant States and countries, and the days spent in the woods with dog and gun are enjoyed even now with a boyish enthusiasm. It is many years since I have shot at a sitting game-bird, and it will be a great many more before I do it again. There is a grand feeling of pride in being able to kill the "hurtling grouse" as he dashes forth from the brush in front of the well-trained setter; and a pleasure that would be marred by the presence of a murdered bird in the game-pocket.

Some of your correspondents are skeptical about the existence of sportsmen who delight in having a ruffed grouse do his very worst when he bursts away through the thicket, but your humble servant is one of the number who does enjoy such shooting the best. A few of my friends will tell you that I am a good shot, but the aforesaid friends are kindly persons who only look at the bag of birds after a day's shooting, and do not count the empty shells. There is an interesting story in many of these empty shells, and I would prefer that it remain untold.

In your last issue "Octo" says that in fifty-four flying shots at grouse he has killed sixteen birds. I have counted shells often enough to know what that means. There have been days when eight or ten empty shells represented as many ruffed grouse in my bag; and there have been other days when the same number of shells would indicate only a bird still in the future. I can show you men, though, who can and do average one bird to every two shots, but they are market shooters, who pick out only the fairest chances, and thereby save an amunition bill. "Octo" probably shoots at all of the birds that rise within range, and so do I, and ten to one we have the most fun. "Octo," I 'm sorry that you killed those two sitting birds. If you can keep up your average on wing shots, come over to our side of the fence, and your virtue will be its own reward.

MY WHITE VIOLET.

LITTLE white violet you are my love,
    Nestling so modestly down in the moss.
  Shyly you hide from the bold sun above,
Humble the home that the oak shadows cross,
Yet 't is the one of your choice, dainty love.

Pretty white violet you are my own,
    Here on the leaves I will lie by your side.
Happy am I at not being alone,
    Never a feeling or mood need I hide
When I am with you, my pure one, my own.

Honest white violet you'll not deceive,
    Nor do I ask you to give love for mine.
Comfort enough 't is for me to believe,
    Pleasure to feel that you cannot design,
Then when I love you, you will not deceive.

AN EASTER CROCUS.

I WATCHED a budding crocus
   As it rose to meet the light,
   From a slumber 'neath the snowbanks
Through the dreary winter night,
And it seemed too bright and lovely
For a thing with roots in dirt.

Came a whisper from Ostâra :
   Stored-up forces from the sun
Sprang from out that bulb all potent—
   And its mission was begun.
For it pleased men with true beauty,
Though the roots were deep in dirt.

Then I thought of Easter morning,
   When a man divine arose,
Calling forth a power eternal
   For believers ; to disclose
All the sin and human folly
That we slumber in, as dirt.

And to-day from all that 's worldly
   May fine character arise
Out of envies, lies, injustice.
   There 's to us a glad surprise
That such thing can spring from forces
Hidden in the midst of dirt.

THE EMPTY KENNEL.

ON the kennel floor the chain lies
　　Where it lay a year ago
　　Rusty, knotted, wound in cobweb,
Where cold spiders hide below.
Creaking on its unused hinges
　　Swings the loose door to and fro,
And the kennel straw is mildewed
　　Dampened by the sifting snow.

Now there is no dog to care for,
　　Silence only when I call,
But I must call : Grouse ! My beauty !
　　Hark ! A moan behind the wall.
Listen ! was that not his voice then ?
　　Moans the wind there—that is all.
Sighs the wind about the kennel
　　While the rustling dead leaves fall.

When the autumn leaves were falling,
　　Just one year ago to-day,
Grouse, the noblest of the setters,
　　Listened in the morning's gray

Till he heard my footsteps coming.
  Leaping sprang at me in play.
Shook his sides and barked so gladly,
  Said to me all he could say.

And he told me that he loved me,
  Said he wanted to obey,
Said he knew just where a partridge
  Hidden 'neath the windfall lay.
There he pointed, staunch as granite,
  While the bold bird dared to stay :
Brought the shot bird back so proudly,
  Asked if that was not the way.

Then I praised the dear old setter,
  Looked down at his earnest eyes,
'Til we felt like two good fellows,
  Bound by all the hunter's ties.
And I said to him : now Grousie,
  Many a year before us lies,
Many a day we 'll hunt together
  Ere the soul of either flies.

So we ranged along together,
  Over meadow, ridge and swale ;
In the swamp the twittering woodcock
  In the brush the calling quail,
Found their hiding spots discovered,
  Found their tricks of no avail.
All in vain the running partridge
  Tried to throw us off his trail.

The Empty Kennel.

When at noon we stopped a moment,
  At the spring beneath the pine,
If he put his nose in first there,
  His was just as good as mine.
For we shared nice things together,
  On the moss we 'd drink and dine.
Side by side our single shadow
  Made a pretty friendship sign.

Late that day the slanting sunbeams
  Reddened all the rocky hill,
With a strange unnatural lighting,
  Colors boding something ill.
Through the forest sped a rabbit,
  Tempting me to try my skill,
'T was no rabbit, but a spirit,
  Some foul thing I could not kill.

Soon its evil work was ended.
  Grouse came slowly back to me,
Looked up at me, asked a question,
  Laid his head against my knee.
On his neck there was a blood stain,
  But no mortal eye could see
What the wound was—how it came there,
  Boy ! asked I, what can this be ?

What is this my bonnie setter ?
  Why do you my presence seek ?
'T is not true that I have harmed you,
  Oh ! if you could only speak.

Tell me if you think I meant it,
  Tell me not in manner meek,
Hurt me not with your forgiveness,
  But on me quick vengeance wreak.

Said he : " Master if you did it,
  Then I know it must be right,
I have been a true companion,
  Worked and loved with all my might.
If from you I should receive this,
  Then my dying pains are light ;
If my day has brought you pleasure,
  Gladly pass I into night."

Tenderly I laid him out then
  On a golden wood-brake sheaf,
Made for him a brilliant covering
  Of the sumac's scarlet leaf.
Sadly left him with the Dryads,
  Asked of them to share my grief :
Faithful friend of man—the setter,
  Dead—with friend of nymph—the leaf.

On the kennel floor the chain lies
  Where it lay a year ago ;
Rusty, knotted, wound in cobweb,
  Where cold spiders hide below.
Creaking on its unused hinges,
  Swings the loose door to and fro,
And the kennel straw is mildewed
  Dampened by the sifting snow.

THE OLD-SQUAW.

ALL the coast in white is covered
    Dark-limbed pines snow burdens bear
    Sea rocks growing thick with fucus
Hide beneath an icy glare !

Out beyond, the waves are surging,
    Darkly, slowly, changing form
While the sea-breeze lulled and quiet
    Waits the coming of the storm.

See the snow-flakes light descending,
    Floating down from leaden sky.
Listen ! o'er the waves a sound comes,
    Ah-ar-luk, the old-squaw's cry.

Low and mellow comes an answer
    From the flock out in the bay,
And the swift bird hears the greeting,
    Turns and throws aloft the spray.

Warm his feathers, cheery-hearted,
    What cares he for wintry cold ?
Gay companion always welcomed,
    Feelings all in singing told.

Ah-ar-luk, as snow is falling,
  Clearly rings o'er all the bay ;
And the voices, floating shoreward
  Chant their love for such a day.

WHAT I FOUND IN THE HUNT-
ING-COAT POCKET.

IN my house there 's a half-hidden closet
    Just under the stairs to the loft,
  And cobwebs are safe in its corners,
  For none of the hands that are soft
Ever dare touch the latch that will open
    To cartridge belts, shotguns, and dangers.
But old Don and I have a feeling
    Of pity for all the poor strangers
To things that are hung on those walls.

There 's a pair of big boots in one corner,
    And snipe decoys, rods and a float ;
But dearest of all the odd things there,
    To me, is the soiled canvas coat.
And to-day in the hunting-coat pocket
    I find a dry, shrivelled-up leaf,
A feather that once was a woodcock's,
    And one little twig, come to grief.
There 's some rabbit hair too, and loose grass-seed.

How quickly for alders of autumn
    My thoughts leave this hot summer day,
For frost-covered corn-shocks and stubble,
    And windrows of brown leaves—and gay,

That rustle to partridge and hunter.
　　The black duck springs quacking from sedges
That shelter the muskrat and mink,
　　And visions of rough, craggy ledges
Are all in plain view in my closet.

The freedom that makes a man noble
　　And draws him from sordid desires
Has come to me here for a moment,
　　And stays while a wood-sprite inquires
If the seeker for fame and a fortune
　　Who wrecks both his body and mind,
Ever gains at the end of the struggle
　　A treasure as rich as I find
In the twig, and the leaf, and the feather.